CW00505858

UNFORGIVEN VICTIMS

ROB PIERCE

Copyright (C) 2024 Rob Pierce

Layout design and Copyright (C) 2024 by Next Chapter

Published 2024 by Next Chapter

Edited by Elizabeth N. Love

Cover art by Lordan June Pinote

This book is a work of fiction. Names, characters, places, and incidents are the product of the author's imagination or are used fictitiously. Any resemblance to actual events, locales, or persons, living or dead, is purely coincidental.

All rights reserved. No part of this book may be reproduced or transmitted in any form or by any means, electronic or mechanical, including photocopying, recording, or by any information storage and retrieval system, without the author's permission.

*For my family: Nathan McWilliams, Julian Pierce, Susan McWilliams,
my brothers Dave and Matt*

*And my friends: Tom Pitts, Joe Clifford, Shawna Yang Ryan, Kate
Thornton, Steve Slany, Liz Buchter, Renee Pickup, Holly West, Mike
Monson, John Mitchell, Grace Emanuel, Warren Lutz, Sean Craven,
Tammy Chalala, Kris Calvin, you know, all y'all and then some.*

*…and everyone I'm accidentally leaving out—I didn't mean it, I
swear!*

Preferring perfect strangers to the company of friends
Because strangers are so easily forgotten

KRIS KRISTOFFERSON, DUVALIER'S
DREAM

BOOK ONE

CHAPTER 1
SHERILEE

THEY SAY I KILLED OTTO WORKMAN. I WAS HIS LOVER, THE natural suspect, and a witness said the killer looked like me. Later the witness changed his mind, and people wondered why. Three years after my acquittal I remain accused, not absolved.

I drink my coffee at an outdoor table, Cinzano umbrella overhead, the only patron outside, my sanity perhaps doubted by those indoors as warm rain falls on this false Europe. I sit in my own falsehood, hair blonde and summer dress bright, sunglasses off, everything different and vision blurred, forever blurred, in and by this my home, where I hide in the open, not seeing people, watching my city in all its unfamiliarity.

This is the place that has only now returned to me after three years absence. This is San Francisco through sober half-blind eyes, a sobriety enforced by sadness so strong that the usual joyous drinking would surely be fatal. And my reaction to this hairpin turn may be how my life is saved, or it may be how the lights go out, slowly dimming, the hazy vision perhaps the clearest I've had, and certainly the best I can have right now.

Once I could sleep and escape, for however weak I felt there was strength in my subconscious. That was before Otto's murder. Now my dreams abound with harsh terror, placing in

3

my hands a pistol all too comfortable, like a thin leather glove and the fingers must be flexed. So I lie awake at night as long as I can and finally pass out, to sleep badly, knowing as I drift off that there will be no mercy in sleep. Awake I am safer, saner; dreams distort the possibilities again and again. I know what I did and didn't do and am unable to accept it.

And now I've returned to my adopted home, but I don't know if it wants me back. I often walk, with nowhere to go, or ride a bus, hidden in the crowd. I do not drive, my car is in storage, the smallest traffic violation would bring out that old driver's license, with that old picture on it and that name—Sherilee Malcolm—I want no one to hear. It is not Otto's name that I hide from but my own, and yes his death haunts me but so does my life. And it is not me but what people think of me.

If people must know me let them read what I once wrote, and from those personae attempt to find whoever I may have been. For I am not that person now, although she of course remains; knowing I must change, in my isolation I attempt to wriggle free.

My problem is not that my life has ended with his, or that I cannot speak his name—I say it over and over, but only to myself, no one else need hear it, no one else need think of him, not the ways that I must.

And when the wind blows, hurling rain in my direction, if I am still writing I will join the crowd inside and continue; if my thoughts are temporarily complete I will stride into the downpour. I have no fear of being drenched. My notebook will be well protected inside my purse.

CHAPTER 2
WASH AND SIMON

I knocked on Hutcheson's door and was gruffly ordered in, something worse than usual in his gravelly voice. I stepped in slowly and made sure the door shut tight behind me. The old man's eyes remained on the file lying open on his desk. I stood, waited to be invited to sit, wanted to find out what was up and get it over with. Hands behind my back, eyes on the wall clock, I assured myself it had only been two minutes. Finally Hutcheson shut the file, opened another, and told me to sit down.

His desk was tidy except for the stack of manila folders before him. An ashtray, dusted clean, sat within my reach, spotless, but it probably always had been. Hutcheson didn't smoke and I doubted any guest would dare sully his air. It was a small office in an old building, one where the windows still opened, and the old man kept one that way as long as the weather permitted.

Chilled, I said nothing. Hutcheson's thick white eyebrows arched up the long slope of his forehead. He looked into my eyes as he looked into everyone's, solemnly, as though probing the mind behind them.

"You've done some good work for the agency, Shank. You work well in the field." He coughed the dust free from his throat.

5

"Yet I hesitate to pull you from your paperwork, which is sometimes, ah, lax."

His nose reminded me of a hawk, and I knew this pause between sentences was not an invitation to speak but a circling before he swooped.

"There are those who think me too old to hesitate before making a decision." He held up one hand in a reflexive gesture dating back to the days when someone might have questioned his word. "But what I am too old for is mistakes." His brow wrinkling down toward his nose, the old man leaned forward, let me in on a grave secret. "I may not have time to correct them. Now I find time is pressing, at least in this matter, and an incorrect decision, at this stage, can be no more disastrous than none."

I nodded my head, like I knew what he was talking about.

His glance did not acknowledge my reaction. "You are the best operator available for this assignment. You will handle it."

The old man slid a folder across the desk. "And, Shank. Be careful this time. Carelessness put us in this mess."

Hutcheson retrieved the file he'd been reading when I entered. He opened it, leaned forward so that I faced the top of his balding dome. I sat there an uneasy couple of seconds, then picked up the file and stood, waited another second, turned and walked out of Hutcheson's office.

With one hand I shut the door behind me while with the other I opened the folder. At the top of the first page was the witness's name: Simon Parker. He had been nineteen at the time, an art student. I wondered at the old man's words: what mistake of mine had kept this case alive?

It had been three years since I'd tracked down Parker at the Art Institute, followed him when he left his class and entered the cafeteria two minutes after he did. Three years since I'd carried a sketch pad, bought a cup of coffee and searched the room for the tall boy's sand-colored hair.

He sat alone at one end of a long table, his own sketch book in front of him, coffee cup near his left hand, and sprawled awkwardly out of the little chair, even seated his height as obvious as his youth.

Parker looked up at me pulling out the chair across from his. I sat and took a cautious sip of my hot coffee. It wasn't worth a grimace but I gave it one anyway, made sure he saw me. "Not very good, is it?"

Parker's pencil hovered an inch above his pad, scribbled lines and circles in the air, stopped. "You get used to it."

"Hope I don't have to. You go to school here?"

His eyes found mine for the first time. "Don't you?"

"Nah," I grinned. "I met a girl here for lunch. A friend fixed us up. Sometimes you wonder who your friends are."

Parker tipped his head to one side and his empty hand flopped open, toward me. "Then the sketch pad?"

"Oh, this." I held up the pad, flipped through its empty pages. "A prop. To let the girl impress me."

"But she's gone, right? And you're still here."

I shook my head. "Do you know what it's like trying to talk to someone like that? I had to get some coffee to wake up enough to leave."

"Mm hm," Parker said, his eyes returning to his paper, curiosity apparently gone.

"My name's Wash Shank."

The odd name seemed to distract him, and his pencil dropped as I reached out and squeezed his hand.

"Simon Parker." I was tall but he was taller, and his hand in mine was more bone than meat, a lot of bone, and I grinned back, thinking this boy, though less than a decade my junior, could be molded.

"Simon Parker?" I squeezed my features together, feigned curiosity. "Have you drawn something famous?"

The boy shook his head. "No, man. I'm a sculptor. But I have been working in mixed media." He said this last part like it was something I needed to know.

"Yeah?" I hoped I looked curious. "Experimental stuff?"

7

"Some of it," Parker answered, brown eyes shining. "I'm trying to find new ways to communicate to a less traditional audience."

"Sounds interesting," I smiled, "but a little vague. Could I see some of it?"

"None of my new stuff's ready yet. I don't like to show works in progress."

I sipped my coffee while Parker talked, set it down when he paused. "I still know your name from somewhere."

I was reluctant to push, but if I didn't Parker would soon rush off.

"Wait!" I said excitedly. "Weren't you the witness in the Otto Workman murder?"

His head snapped back. "How do you know about that?"

I shrugged. "I know a lawyer. Word gets out."

Parker's head shook. "Shouldn't." It shook in the opposite direction. "I'm not supposed to talk about it."

"Me neither." I frowned, waited.

"You?" He blinked. "You were there?"

"No," I shook my head, still frowning. "It's a different murder I'm not supposed to talk about."

Parker's pencil loosened in his fingers. He laid it gently on the table, like it was wounded.

"Look," I said, "I knew you were a student here. And neither of us is supposed to talk, right? I figured you were one person I could talk to."

Parker nodded.

I held up an open hand. "It's so hard to never tell anyone. I swear I'll go nuts."

Parker nodded again. Then he smiled, knowingly. "Are you gay? Is this a pickup?"

"This is San Francisco. Would I go to all this trouble?" I leaned back. "I need to talk."

"Yeah," Parker said, picking up his pencil. "I know."

It was a twenty-minute walk to Parker's apartment, or so he said, not explaining how fast that walk would be.

"I like to walk," he said, charging forward. "That's how I saw the murder." His voice dropped but his steps didn't slacken. "I left the Institute around five or six. I saw the shooting about eight-thirty or nine." His head bobbed a little, too fast for me to tell if he shook it. "Most people don't like to walk that much, I know. But I like the city, and I spend the whole day in one place. Sometimes you have to keep walking until you're in the middle of the picture."

Parker's eyes moved everywhere, attempted to see everything, his long, fast strides threatening to hurtle him past it all. The constant motion made it easy to believe him as he spoke of his restlessness, his need to work in more than one medium, to communicate more immediately with the world. I didn't understand all his art terminology, but he did convince me of his need for immediacy. Although I was nearly his height, and our legs about the same length, I strained to keep pace. I took a deep breath and checked my watch when we at last reached the five-story building he lived in. It had been only twenty minutes. Of course, Parker lived on the top floor. Of course, we took the stairs.

His head held high, his body moved with a previously unseen grace, as though he now stood in splendor. Parker led me into the living room of his two-bedroom apartment, an apartment he shared, he explained, with a friend whose hours were as odd as his own. He expected we would be alone or joining a crowd, for it was far too early for his roommate to come home empty-handed.

The little rectangular living room was cramped, with small plants and sculptures defining the perimeters, most of these space fillers sitting close enough to the ground that I could peer through their leaves and branches, through their arms and other limbs less easily described, and gaze upon the plethora of paintings most notable not for any artistic qualities but for how little space was permitted to squeeze between them. The array ran floor-to-ceiling along each wall, not something to be looked at except by the unavoidable glares of malignant strangers.

If the shrinking feeling inside me had gravitated to my exterior, it did not mar my host's happiness with my reaction. Indeed he looked proud, waved me with aplomb to a seat on a couch I hadn't seen, offered me one of the beers I'd bought on the way over. I accepted. The air was clean with the scent of the plants, but there were too many of them, there was too much of everything. Parker and his friend had taken a living room and turned it into a storage locker.

Unfamiliar faces filled the room. These paintings and photographs and sculptures were not real, did not look real. They were screams, and causes of screams; the nightmares that awaken. And I did not see a single face, but a mass of them, as though I were the only human on an alien planet.

"How do you like it?" the boy asked, pulling a large, wooden rocking chair across the room to a spot facing me. He slipped into it.

I took a long drink of beer and sank back into the couch. "The beer or the room?"

Parker shrugged his scraggy shoulders. "Either one."

"I'd drink a lot of beer if this was my room."

"We do. Something you don't like about it?"

It was my turn to shrug. "Think you could cram a few more things in here?"

"The living room is this way because we like it this way. Did you want to see some of my sculptures?"

"I can see plenty from here."

"Would you like to compare any of them to photographs of the models?"

"No, they seem quite realistic," I deadpanned, glancing at the dozens of grotesque faces looking at me. "The ones that are supposed to, that is."

"They're all supposed to," Parker answered. "Sometimes reality comes in a dream."

Fucking artist, I thought, but kept it to myself, wanting to redirect the conversation. "Or a nightmare. The killing I saw…"

"Yeah?"

I sipped at my beer, not smiling but pleased as the boy leaned forward to listen. I pulled a pint of Jack Daniel's from a coat pocket, broke the seal, and took a drink. I passed him the bottle.

"He was right in front of me."

I waited for Parker to say 'wow' or something, but he sat quiet, fingers wrapped around the pint, eyes on me, mouth slightly open.

"It was one of those crowded little streets in Chinatown, you know, hard to move and half the people are five feet tall and eighty years old, can't get out of the way."

Parker nodded twice, blinked, urged me on.

"I was headed to North Beach, and I like the sights in Chinatown, all that crap the tourists love I love too. So I wasn't paying attention where I was going and wind up on this block filled with Chinese. I'm barely able to move and I realize, the Chinese don't even think this is crowded. So I weave my way through the traffic, hear this yelling all the way, know I'm moving toward it but hey, what am I gonna do, turn around? And when I reach the corner, these two guys are yelling at each other, young guys in nice suits. I figure I'll walk past this, they're yelling in English, motherfucker this and motherfucker that, and as I'm coming outta the crowd I get pushed in the back and go stumbling forward a few steps, as the one guy yanks a blade from his coat and buries it in the middle of the other guy's gut."

I paused for a breath, and a drink. Parker's eyes were wide, one hand frozen holding the beer where it sat on the chair arm. With the other hand, he threw a rapid slug of Jack Daniel's into his mouth. Gradually he'd leaned forward as my story unfolded, until now he was bent into a full-fledged hunch. His mouth hung open enough for his tongue to fit between his lips. I drank until he licked them.

"So the guy who gets stabbed falls into me, and I go down to my knees while he grabs the top of my head. When I look up, he's reaching into his coat and he pulls out a pistol. The other guy pulls the knife free and swings it back up. The bleeding guy pulls the trigger. Time stops, I swear to God. I'm shaking, the kick from the gun runs right through my body. I'm there on my knees, and all I can hear is this high-pitched scream. You'd never think it was a man. And I see the knife hit the sidewalk and bounce. Then there's another shot. It feels like I'm in an earthquake. And the guy drops."

Parker drank beer, then whiskey, leaned back slightly. I watched him watch me, watched him breathe deep.

I lowered my voice. "Then the guy with the gun falls to his knees and laughs. He stays there a minute, not laughing anymore. He breathes heavy, gets up and runs. Right into North Beach, the bottom of his shirt black with blood."

"And the guy he shot? Did he die right away?"

"That's what they said." I shook my head, lowered my eyes. I returned my gaze to the boy's face, paused before his hooked-fish mouth. I shook my head again, blinked, looked him square in the eye.

Parker was still, except to swallow. For a minute all his concentration went to that. I wondered what he was thinking, what his next question would be. I waited for that swallow to finish.

"When do you testify?" he finally choked out.

I laughed. "Testify?" I shook my head.

Parker looked confused. "But someone has to testify."

"Maybe someone who isn't afraid of death. Or Florida. Death or relocation, witness protection, they take away your life somehow. Not for me. I like living. In San Francisco."

We both drank, and I thought about what I was going to say next while I watched Parker absorb the beer and my bullshit.

I waved an empty hand slowly across the air, a referee signaling illegal motion. "You should've seen the dead man right before the trigger was pulled. The knife was in mid-swing when he saw the gun. He kept swinging but you could see it in his face. He knew what was coming, and then it came. He didn't have time to think about it. He didn't have time to do anything but die."

I drank, waited for Parker to take his cue.

He saw me looking at him, took another drink from the Jack Daniel's. I licked my lips and smiled. Parker didn't smile back, mumbled to the floor. "It must've been like that for Otto too."

I cleared my throat, leaned forward, half-whispered. "You saw his face?"

Parker blinked, sat back, blinked again, and leaned toward me. "I was the first one to reach the body. But I didn't see anything in his face." He shook his head. "I looked. To see if he looked scared, or surprised."

Parker's fingers moved as he spoke, sculpted small features, but the words had stopped coming out. As though he still knew he wasn't supposed to talk but was pretty sure he was going to. He owed me a story.

My eyes wandered away from Parker's, took a blind, slow stroll around the room. "Did you know him?" I asked softly.

Parker straightened in his chair. "Well, of course I knew who he was. I was a fan. I even met him once."

My eyes widened, my voice dropped again. "You met him? Where?"

"Oh," he said, stretching his neck right then left, "that was nothing but luck. He was doing a book signing at City Lights, which I hadn't heard about but I happened to be there that evening and there he was. I told him how much I admired his work and I shook his hand."

The conversation was drifting, and I had to let it drift. Parker had to believe I cared about Otto Workman.

"What did he say?"

Parker lifted his beer when I began to speak, but my question was short and so was his drink. "He asked me what I did. I didn't know what he meant, so I told him I was a student. He said that's what he was too, but he didn't let it stop him from doing things."

The boy's smile broadened. "Then he asked if I was staying for his talk. I was sick but he asked, so I said yes and I stayed."

In my own face I tried to mirror Parker's excitement, leaned forward to look into his eyes. I stretched my voice a little higher than usual. "God, a man like that—it must have been awful finding his body. And you saw the murder, too?"

"I was the only one who saw it. I was fifty feet away, and it was night, but the sky was clear and the moon full, the street well-lit besides."

Parker looked down but I frowned, a performance for the statues and the pictures on the wall. "A great night for a walk."

Somehow he saw me and frowned back. "It was." His eyes closed and his chin dropped into his chest. His head moved up, slowly with each breath.

Through narrowed eyes I watched him.

His lips trembled, his eyes blinked.

The eyes shut again but the mouth opened this time. I leaned forward for the words dropping slowly toward his chest.

"I was walking uphill, getting my legs good and stretched, and my lungs emptied of the smells of paint and clay. Filling them with air."

"It—" I spoke quietly but his head jerked up in response, his eyes wide, seeing my face so close, "It didn't happen directly in front of you. Did it?"

This was what Parker wasn't supposed to talk about. I could see the silence choking him. His whole face looked pulled back, like he'd had one too many face lifts.

"You're not a reporter, are you?"

"You don't have to tell me," I said, turned my head away. "I don't want you to get in trouble." I drank some beer. "I know what I went through with mine."

Parker looked at me, then down at his beer bottle. "Sorry," he told it. "I—I need to talk, but it's so hard."

"I know," I said. "I'd tell you to relax, but I know what that's like too." I took a drink.

"You do," he said, making it almost a question, turned his head and studied my face. "There was a car parked at the top of the hill, on the far side of the street, facing to my left."

Parker looked down at his beer, swallowed without its help, and looked at me again, his voice low. "There was a flash of light and an explosion from inside the car, and a woman got out and ran down the street."

"And you saw her face?"

"I still see her. Her hair was shoulder length and dark, straight and thin, like her face except her face was white, almost white. A long, thin nose and thin lips."

"You could see her lips in profile?"

Parker hesitated, but only a moment. "No. I remember now. She turned once and looked back, and in that instant I saw her full face. Skin tight, cheekbones high. Her eyebrows were thin, too."

My eyes, already wide, stayed that way. "You caught all that in an instant?"

"You don't believe me?"

It was too soon to show much doubt. "Maybe your eyes are better than mine."

"I'm an artist, Wash. Vision is critical to what I do."

I sipped. "You know you described Sherilee Malcolm."

Parker took another slug of Jack Daniel's. "Of course."

"And you know she and Workman were close."

"I know they were lovers. I don't know if they still are. Still were."

15

Parker took a drink. So did I. The more time his thoughts had to settle the better. Yet it was up to me to prompt him, to get more out of him, and it had to seem natural. I squinted, tried for a pensive look. Finally, I asked, "Did you run to the car when she ran away?"

"Not at first. I waited. For more explosions, I guess. It seemed dark all of a sudden."

I could see him freezing, there on the street and here in the apartment. I stared into a statue's eyes until he spoke again.

"I stood there. I thought the man must've been shot..." He drank the Jack, ignored the beer. "...and the woman must've shot him. So I moved, I must've, but I don't know how fast. Or how long I stood there."

Parker stopped, exhaled deeply, and drank his whiskey, as though he'd told me something he knew he'd have to say to someone someday but wasn't sure he could, and now he thought he'd said it. It may have relieved the boy to release that moment that had been trapped inside him, but it did little for me.

"You don't know if you ran to the car?" I asked.

"I guess I did. But I don't remember doing it."

"Doesn't matter. You got there and you saw what you saw."

"Yeah." Parker was saying more than he was supposed to, and he knew it. But his speech wasn't slurred, though the pint was nearly gone. He was obviously a drinker, but even if he looked sober he couldn't be.

Blurt it out, you bastard. "What was it, Simon? What did you see?"

Parker shook his hanging head. "He was in the driver's seat, blood everywhere. He was dead." The boy gulped, coughed like he'd swallowed wrong. "I tried to check his heartbeat, but that was where the blood came from."

His words had slowed down, probably right behind his mind. Like if he was reluctant to talk it was okay. I didn't care how he felt about it, so long as I heard it all. Sherilee Malcolm was accused in the shooting, and she was our client. There were other details, but without the kid's testimony the prosecution had no case.

"I had to lean through the window over his body. To check. I got some blood on my hand. And I backed up, bumped my head against the door. The car door. And I, I was trying to turn my head then, and I threw up on the steering wheel."

His words halted again. I resisted the impulse to grab one of his statues and bop him over the head with it.

"And?" I said.

"And some of it got on his shirt. I fell forward a little, caught myself, then I checked his pulse. There wasn't any. It was like I thought."

"And you recognized Workman right away."

"Almost immediately."

I held back a grin. "Almost?"

"Not at first. Not before I checked his pulse. But the second time, after I was sure he was dead, yeah."

"Then what happened?"

"I'm not sure. I was shocked. It was worse than the throwing up, seeing who it was. Otto. After I saw his face I don't know what I did. I stayed there, I know that. And," he rubbed the back of his neck, "I think I screamed. They tell me I did anyway."

"They?"

"The police, the doctor. They had me looked at. I was okay. I guess I couldn't talk at first; they didn't know what happened to me. I had all that blood on me."

"On your hand."

"All over. My clothes were a mess. I don't know. After I saw his face, I don't know."

"Man," I said. "Otto. To see him that way. You know, I grew up on his books." I shook my head.

Parker's face turned alert. "You like him too?"

"Hey, I'm not much older than you. I grew up on that shit."

"Yeah," Parker agreed, "his characters always had so much pride. No matter what they did."

17

"And now he's gone. Who'd ever believe Sherilee would've killed him?" I stood. "Let's get some more drinks in here."

The refrigerator filled almost half the tiny kitchen. I returned to the living room with two fresh beers, handed one to Parker.

He blinked like he wasn't sure. "Thanks." He smiled strangely, his mouth barely open. I thought he might issue attack commands to his gargoyles.

We drank our beers. Parker got up and put on some music. Somewhere in that morass of art and nature was a stereo. A tenor sax played slow, soft.

"You know," Parker returned to his chair, "I'm doing her face." His words were barely audible. His eyes blinked, attempted to brighten, and his slumped shoulders straightened.

"You're doing her face?" I was too damned sure I understood.

"Only sketches so far—"

"But I thought you were through with sculpture."

"This is only an exercise, something for me."

"You're going to sculpt her face."

"Yeah, the way I saw it that night."

"The way you saw it after you knew who the dead man was?"

"The way I saw it. Turned back my way. Facing me. The white face thin, everything thin. Her head bobbing as she ran, but for that one instant, still. Frozen."

"Frozen."

"Frozen."

We were repeating ourselves at a point in the conversation when the subject had not yet changed his mind, still believed what he could not, what it was my job to prevent him from believing. I had to turn the conversation back to my business, and away from his.

"I think it's interesting," I said, and drank some beer.

"What?"

"You saw the woman before you saw the dead man, right?"

18

"Yeah."

"And she was running away, you were sure she was the killer."

"Yeah."

"And you know who Sherilee Malcolm is, you'd recognize her if you saw her. But with your trained, observant, artist's eyes, you didn't see Sherilee Malcolm running away. You didn't think of her until you saw the dead man was Otto Workman."

I looked at Parker and he looked at the floor, and all the faces he'd sculpted joined me in looking at him. He kept looking down. When he finally lifted his head it was to tilt back his bottle. He finished the beer like it was his only friend. Still without a word, without a glance in my direction, he stood, walked to the kitchen, and came back with two more beers, handed me one, looked at me only then.

Parker turned off the stereo and we polished off the beer without speaking. He was confused, doubting himself, and that was good. But I also doubted, doubted I had convinced him, and, the night reduced to silence, would leave him knowing my job was not finished.

CHAPTER 3
SHERILEE

THE RAIN LET UP, BUT I WAS ALREADY WET. SAN FRANCISCO RAIN, once glorious, a thing that might clean a lesser city's streets. As though unkempt sidewalks were a source of pride, a requirement of the decadence in which I once reveled. Yet where I was no longer seemed to matter, I no longer saw the details that once made this place so special; the city I loved was a table in the rain.

I could be anywhere now, for wherever I was I would be absent. I was not here, here was not here. "If it's all the same to you" had ceased to be a meaningless phrase, instead had become startlingly accurate—everywhere was the same to me, everyone was the same. I had traveled, and discovered nothing. I met strangers and they were all nothing, people I didn't know and wouldn't know. The experiences I'd been accumulating did not increase me, did not reduce me; things occurred in my presence, but they did not happen *to me*. Even the rain altered only my exterior.

My clothes were soaked through, and there was no color but gray on that canvas of clouds. Yet I had enough money for a cab or, if I could not flag one, the nearest hotel, making this not only not a disaster but preferable to inertia, any problem to be solved a fortuitous distraction. Thus my laugh, which in its volume and my solitude must have seemed that of a madwoman, was but a reasonable acknowledgment of irony by the beleaguered.

I walked past hotels I could have taken, wet as I was, determined to return to the room I rented by the week; a monthly rate had been offered but seemed too great a commitment. It wasn't the unaffordability of something nearer that delivered my drenched body back to its point of departure, but the need for a change of clothes. A shower and two towels to wear for the remainder of the night would be an endurable but unnecessary limit. I had no plans to leave my room, but neither did I wish to be imprisoned there.

Once in the door I poured myself a small glass of bourbon and drank it, then poured a tall one and got undressed. I set the full glass on the bedside table and stepped into the shower.

The table wasn't big enough to use as a desk, it was one of those little hotel jobs with the Bible inside. But I could sit up in bed and work, and the table could hold my drink. Hell, my first book was written mostly in a car. Where I sat had nothing to do with how little I wrote.

But I hadn't been writing lately and I needed to. If those brief but exhilarating times with Otto came back hauntingly I should be able to write them, if not for publication then for catharsis, but what had been coming instead were images not words, not that I could write down, not about reality, but small fragments of a picture that had been shredded and strewn.

I had seen puzzles made of images before, of course; I grew up in the sixties, I did acid and Beatles and Hendrix and Stones, and Janis like every good girl should, i even did a bit of cummings. And the awakenings of my youth had included death: friends murdered by war, acquaintances by cops, heroes by drugs. But it had been years, and I didn't do new things anymore. I suppose I had settled on what I wanted. And Otto was part of that.

I would like to mourn him with words but too often they will not come, a specter envelops me and all I have is madness. I

21

cannot write I cannot think, my mind is filled with thoughtless fury, and I know it is my fault he is dead, and I know nothing else matters, although it cannot be my fault, it *is* not, but I cannot stand and scream and have it gone, I cannot sit and scribble, I cannot make sacrifices to the minotaur or the volcano, this world is unchangeable. And, not being a tragic heroine, I see no reason to leave it.

We went to bed in the neighborhood of midnight; we didn't sleep until much later. Kept awake not by romance, or even sex, but insomnia: ruler of the night and of the dawn.

That night, lying awake in bed, Otto beside me, I could not sleep and I could not get up and write. I sensed that he too remained awake, yet I could not think of a word to say, we had said too much already. It was not drunkenness that kept us together, we did not drink that way; first there was yelling, then maybe some breaking of glass, and eventually one of us would storm out, the last few drinks to be downed in the solitary turmoil some call peace. Under such circumstances we would part, to pursue other facets of our lives. We could not stay together when we argued, but that night we did, and, rare as it was that insomnia would set upon us both without either of us rising to write or read, that night it did. Perhaps our thoughts were too muddy for even a muse to shine through. Perhaps it was too early for sleep. Still, it was odd that I did not get up to pour myself a nightcap, odd that I chose this moment to turn around and reach for Otto, odder still that he chose the same moment to turn and reach for me. In this unique set of circumstances we made love, until exhausted we fell asleep in each other's arms. This was the night before he died.

Now he is gone, never to return. And those who believed me guilty will always believe me guilty. Yet the blame that is mine has nothing to do with the beliefs of others; the guilt I feel is independent of logic, of reality as can be seen or touched. Innocence is supposed to have something to do with purity, a thing I lost in infancy if I had it even then. But it is since Otto's death that I have lost whatever part of me was closest to innocent, lost a naïveté I didn't know I possessed. I no longer see the world I live in. Every place is strange, every person a stranger. This world I find myself in is neither round nor flat, is nothing that has been discovered, not exactly. And it's hard to say where I've been. Not that I don't know, but I don't want to tell. Place names may seem an odd secret to cling to, but they are a part of the me who tried to get away, when I tried to become something ambient instead of someone involved. Unless you've been this shattered, you don't know where I am. There is a precision here that cannot be described, that does not fit within the established parameters: a precision that stabs, then twists.

Cold morning breeze upon my bare arms, it is weather I expect and bask in. Better a cutting wind and temporary discomfort than perfect weather and the perfect people it attracts. I like mine slightly chilled, thank you, like champagne. And I do not wonder at their popping corks, rather that there are not more of them, for explosions of anger and exuberance are lives not resigned to mediocrity. I find a little café, order a coffee and a croissant, sit alone at a small table, and watch the door for admirers or anyone else who might know me.

It is odd, this quiet dining, this no one but me, this absence of others and rage within. Tumult I find, incoherence, and remember when those elements were provided by the disjointed jabbering of wits, the clever rejoinders of simultaneous dialogues, the occasional conversation developing against odds. I never had difficulty talking trash with the boys, years of waitressing and other resentments built up, but I rarely saw the point. So I would get drunk, and see another point altogether, one that may not have been there but was visible to me, and I batted my eyes and smoked their cigarettes and fucked their wives, like they did. And there was glory in that. There truly was.

Perhaps I have sometimes had to play the games of others to find my own strength, but that step is preferable to many another. I do not regret those years, I do not consider that time wasted, although the repetitions of the scene may have become formulaic, that most dreaded of words (next to plagiaristic) for one attempting to find originality. For I enjoyed those games, and never saw them as more, and knew that certain pleasures might have heavy payments later. But not for Otto. Even if he had lived that way, he did not live long enough to pay for his physical indulgences. Unless the woman who killed him was one of those.

My guess is it was emotional and mental excess that did him in, and if she was a lover, I wonder why she looked like me.

Murder: one life gone, innumerable others altered. The killer, the victim's friends, acquaintances, anyone he touched. Anyone either touched. And, of course, Otto's book sales skyrocketed, as did mine. Makes you feel good about your audience, bunch of vultures. So what good has the work done, if these are the people it is reaching? And are agents and publishers now urging other writers to kill each other?

Murder murder murder, the word beats in my brain as I sip my coffee and glare at the strangers sauntering through the café door, people I don't know and don't want to know.

I sit alone and tremble, feel the tremor in my chest. Perhaps I will die soon, have my life cut short—that is, shorter than expected, if no shorter than fate could allow—and am I prepared for an afterlife, if there is one, or is what I require to be strong something unavailable beyond the grave? Perhaps there is nothing, and what is that like? What can nothing be?

I tremble again, chomp on doughy pastry, and wash it down with a gulp of coffee. This is not relaxing, the presence and absence of strangers who do and do not walk through the door.

Otto, a short man with large hands, clamps one down on my shoulder and I rise from my chair. He is not behind me of course, but I feel his presence and am comforted as I walk slowly, head not turning, out the door and onto the sidewalk.

Smiling shyly, to him and to myself, I turn around, reenter the café, remove two dollars from my purse and set the tip on the table.

I leave again, alone but nothing wrong with that. Peace, for however short a time, is with me.

The pain relievers of different generations: jazz and pot and booze for the beats, rock and pot and acid by the time I came along. Otto came somewhere between, and was prone to mix and match. And I had discovered the glories of alcohol early, as a teenager on the run, taking all the pleasures I could.

And among those reliefs let's not forget Buddhism, or whatever elements of it and other Eastern religions fit into each group's respective belief systems.

My acceptance of all else left little room for religion, even if it wasn't the kind I was raised on. Otto, as a Kerouac connoisseur, had little choice; Zen Catholicism loomed. In my desperation to survive as I wanted, that was not the type of rebellion that could present itself as a choice. Religion was something my father had, and no logic can ever change the way I feel about that. Religion is for men like him, spiteful men who must control all they can, as though they were the live incarnations of that God they claim to believe in. It is not difficult for me to believe there is a Godlike creature out there somewhere; it is impossible for me to believe there is a God that could fit within the limits of such a man's comprehension.

It wasn't because I was pregnant that I left home when I was fourteen. I could've gotten the abortion and gone back. But Small Town, U.S.A., was nothing to go back to. I needed something that wasn't there, and I had to get away from what was. Home was no home and I believed in Paradise. Or at least that there had to be something better. So Steven and I borrowed his dad's car and never took it back.

We dumped the car as soon as we could and got another one, beat up and cheap. I don't know if anyone knew old Fords well enough to make that thing purr, but Steven got it mobile and that was what we needed. No one was chasing us; we were running. It was 1970 and we were wild and so was the anti-war pro-drugs pro-love counterculture. Nixon was such an obvious enemy, the evil father too many of us had. The problem was the heroes had begun to die. Not people like John Kennedy; I was only seven when he was shot, his death meant nothing to me. He was no savior anyway but a politician, a symbol of an era that for many of us never existed. The nation I grew up in already wore a shadow across its innocence. Dire times required magical salvation, a beauty nonexistent in the real world of TV news and adult solutions. I found the beauty and rebellion I required in the music and persona of Jimi Hendrix. And in 1970 Jimi Hendrix died. Gone almost as soon as he had come. Jimi was twenty-seven when he died, not quite twice my age, and it crossed my mind more than once that I might be halfway done. I'd been lost so long, and found so briefly. The diaries I'd kept for years were no longer enough to hold the words that exploded from me, and the new words, powered by death, meant too much to me not to be shared.

Some say I grew up poetic, but at some point you grow up. I'd always been a bad girl in somebody's eye, and now I wore that badness like a badge. Obsessed with writing, I waitressed my way to New York, left Steven behind. When I finally got

26

published, I was promptly labeled a "New York" writer, so I left. I moved to San Francisco and stayed, with frequent returns to New York, and so-called vacations getting away from cities and people, vacations spent getting indignant and yelling at people, telling them who I was. My name is Sherilee Malcolm, dammit. I'm a published author. One of the few things in this world I could imagine wanting to be. And the little towns didn't care, as I should have known they wouldn't, except for the occasional rebel on his or her way out. I need cities and people, even if they sometimes bore me.

So now I'm what I've always needed to be, the bohemian poet intellectual whore half the world dreads and the other half craves. Or maybe the same half. And now they say I've shot someone. To further whet all appetites.

Before I met Otto my books sold okay, the reviews were generally good, and some people seemed afraid of me. All of that was fine. I liked my little scene and I was its queen. People called me 'The Black Widow' behind my back; I liked that too.

In *Journal of a Bitch* I mentioned my veneration for Otto and his work, both as a novelist and as a political activist. I was hardly the first person to speak highly of Otto, but I was one of the few to receive his public approval. I was giving a reading at San Francisco State, and I didn't even know Otto was there until I was leaving and, turning away from the podium, was met by his embrace.

Cameras flashed and we made the eleven o'clock news. Otto was *that* famous. One hug got me more press than had my entire career up to that time. People began to pay attention. The new reviews were bigger than the old. *A Woman's Place Is in Your Face*, published six months earlier, leapt onto best seller lists. And there was a bidding war for my next novel, *Stacked on the Inside*. All prompted by a hug. Otto and I became lovers.

Otto Workman wrote about what it was like to be poor and hungry and proud; his novels brought to their pages lives of struggle, bodies in pain and boredom and grasping at pleasure. It was life as it was, sometimes becoming life as it was supposed to be, sometimes not. His protagonists were hard-working men, often men who hated their jobs but saw no way out of them, sometimes men who saw a chance to escape that drudgery and desperately took that chance. And they were usually men you wouldn't mind having a beer with, although they weren't all good drunks.

I'm not always a good drunk either, and I like to drink. Otto also was known to take one or two in his spare time, the difference being that I seemed to have much more spare time than he did. Otto was always in motion, organizing a rally then dashing to a quick appearance at a fundraiser, making a speech here and leading a march there. But when he stopped long enough to drink with me, we drank until we quarreled and wanted to kill each other, with none of that intelligent debate each of us was so proud of but words which grew more violent, meteoric, untempered by wisdom or mercy, the fuel of alcohol burning from our minds everything but hatred, all the stored-up hatred of our angry fighting lives.

With all the words we had written, we could not find the right ones for each other. Not often enough for the two of us to stay together. All our training was in creating fictions and other people's lives; we were no better prepared for love than was anyone else.

Had we gotten back together prior to Otto's death, or were we seeing each other only as friends? This was the sort of information the public clamored for at the trial, but the only testimony was mine, and I denied the suggestion everyone wanted to believe. No one else could testify with any certainty on the matter, no one else knew. No one would ever know. It was a question of whether they chose to believe me.

And now, three years after the trial, I hear rumors that I'm living overseas, in France or Spain. I did go to Europe for a while, and my movements could easily have stopped in a land where what I'd been accused of could be accepted as an act of passion. Assuming I was guilty, as many people did. But everywhere I revealed myself an explanation was demanded, and protests of innocence could not be accepted by those who wished to forgive me for my guilt. I must have known, as the trial progressed, what lay ahead. When I look now at the old, preserved banner headline—SHERILEE MALCOLM ACQUITTED!—my eyes are drawn to the photograph below, a photograph of myself far from exuberant, a sadness in my face, a sadness not only for Otto but for myself as well.

I reveal myself no more.

CHAPTER 4
WASH AND SIMON

I PLANTED A BUG AND RECORDER IN PARKER'S APARTMENT. MOST OF the dialogue was with his roommate and he didn't have many guests, but when he was alone Parker talked to himself, and words of doubt were central to his vocabulary. He didn't know about this, wasn't sure about that, and although the focus of his confusion was the art he attempted to create, his malleability was easy to see. He was young and involved in things he'd never been involved in before, things involving life and death, things I knew all too well. Simon knew almost nothing, but he had created for himself an illusion of certainty that gave strength to his art, a strength reliant on his perceptions, his ability to see and read a face and body better than other people. And it was my job to cast doubt on those beliefs, to cause the boy to disown his faith. He was young and thought he knew the world, or at least how to perceive it. I was older and my duty was to show him the flaws in all human perceptions, the mistakes the senses convey to the mind. He had to know that not everything he saw was what he thought it was, that everything he remembered he might remember wrong, that the mind altered what it perceived to fit what it understood and that there was much it did not understand.

The red-haired woman who bumped into Simon was five foot three, one hundred ten pounds. Looking straight ahead she'd be facing his lower ribs. She tipped her head back to look at his face.

"Excuse me."

He glanced down, the impact of her bumping him barely noticeable against his bulk. He might have wondered how she walked straight into him in the uncrowded aisle, but he looked down and, absorbed with her face, he did not think at all.

"That's alright," he answered softly, wanting to be better with words, wanting to impress her but not knowing how.

"Excuse me," she said again, "I meant, do you know where the art books are?"

She smiled as though she were imposing on him, but probably knew she was too pretty for anything she asked to be an imposition.

Simon stood there in his paint-stained jeans and looked at what she wore, utilitarian baggy messageless T-shirt and loose black slacks, no fashion trend that he knew of but too pretty for any clothes to make her plain, and he wanted to sculpt her pageboy haircut and slightly rounded face—a hint of baby fat— her bright blue eyes under faint brows and short lashes, her lightly freckled cheeks and her nose like a smoothed arrowhead, wide lips painted several tones softer than her auburn hair.

"Uh yeah," he answered, probably not as quickly as he should have, but her smile didn't fade and neither did his absorption. "Over here," and restrained what seemed a natural impulse to put an arm around her back, instead walked her further down the narrow aisle, high shelves filled with books on either side of them.

"I spend a lot of time in here. Is there something in particular you're looking for?"

He knew he was saying too much, but was afraid of saying

too little, of losing her, and he knew he had asked an open-ended question, which left her more options than he wanted her to have, but he had never been good at picking up strangers, never been good at expressing interest. His interest was too selfish, he wanted her to pose for him and he wanted to have sex with her. But the transparency of his selfishness often caused his baser needs to not be met, and he inwardly cringed at what he had said and hoped her response would somehow allow him to steer the conversation in a less honest direction, one in which his selfishness would not be so obvious.

"Thanks," she smiled up at him, "I'm fine," and he knew he had blown it, he would never have her, as lover or model. So he tried to hold her in his memory, to remember her later and recreate her and thus have her forever anyway, her image at least, a thing that would long outlast the reality of her, at least in his life.

And now he was stuck because he no longer wanted to look at books but was embarrassed by his feeble attempt at a pickup, and did not want to stand here beside her reminding himself of his rejection, wanted her even more knowing he could not have her.

Simon reached down suddenly, pulled a book on sculpture off a low shelf, and began flipping through the pages as casually as he could, tried to slow himself down. He did not want to stand beside her long, but he could not rush away. He caught a glimpse of her browsing the architecture shelves, and forced his eyes down into his book to the photographs he knew too well and the text that would not register, his eyes in one direction, his mind another. Not watching her he still knew she had removed a book from the shelf. She glanced at its cover only briefly and took it under her arm.

"Thanks," she said softly, and was walking away when he looked up.

Surprised, he had to clear his throat to answer, and she moved quickly.

"You're welcome," he half-shouted, awkwardly looking up from the book he held as a prop. He looked at the shelf, not caring about the titles now, not seeing them. He looked where she walked. He liked the way her hips moved and wished he had some excuse to chase after her, wished he'd said nothing stupid while she was here, then smiled admiringly, watched her go. His life, he smiled, was aesthetically better for having seen her once. She moved beyond view, and he shared his smile with the bookshelf before him. He let the book he still held fall shut in one large hand and swung it down along his side. He needed it no more, so quickly returned it to its space on the bottom shelf. And saw, by his feet, an envelope.

He picked it up, it had to be hers. He glanced at the name on the envelope, Jackie O'Connell, that could be her, and he took a long stride in the direction she'd gone. She was already out of the aisle and on the stairs, heading up probably to the cashier, and he did not want to shout either "Miss" or "Jackie," did not want to call attention to himself, he'd overplayed his hand already. So he hurried toward her, certain he could catch her on the stairs. Half-running, at the end of his aisle Simon heard footsteps coming around the corner of the adjoining aisle and he skipped deftly to one side to avoid the collision. It was an old man with a cane: Simon stopped suddenly, dodged him easily, regained his balance, and was about to take another long stride forward when the old man's guide dog jumped at his leg.

Simon leapt back as the large white dog propped its front feet against his thighs and lapped at the air before his crotch.

"Down Roger!" croaked the old man, bringing his cane down on the ground like a god commanding thunder. The dog continued lapping and panting, crazy or happy Simon couldn't tell. Anyway it had its mouth right in front of his dick and who knows what makes a dog happy.

"Roger!" the old man commanded again, bringing his staff down even harder.

The dog, wagging its tail frantically, stood on its hind legs and rested its front paws on Simon's chest, its frenetic tongue darting in and out toward Simon's mouth.

"I'm so sorry," said the old man. "Roger isn't usually like this. He likes you. Not in a sexual way, probably."

Simon gasped and pulled himself back farther from the dog's frenzied tongue.

"He's not trained that way, I mean, even if I was into that, I wouldn't train my guide dog that way—"

"Are you fucking crazy?!!"

"I'm telling you Roger only likes you *platonically.*"

"Will it bite?" Simon asked.

"No, no," the old man laughed, pulling back on Roger's leash.

The dog off his chest, Simon took one step back. "You sure?"

"Of course."

Simon stepped cautiously around the still panting dog and past it, looked back, expecting it to jump him from behind, walked slowly so he wouldn't arouse it, hoped the woman he had been following was stuck in a slow checkout line.

His steps up the stairs were slow but long, and though the dog's eyes followed him up, the creature remained on its haunches. Simon made it to the top of the stairs untouched.

From the top of the stairway, he could see the short line at the cash register. She was not in it. He dashed out the door onto Columbus Avenue, looked left and right and across the street but did not see her, a few people walking and an old Chinese man on the corner shouting to no one in particular. Simon ran to the corner a few feet away, stood beside the Chinese man and looked up and down Broadway but did not see her there either, saw only cars and heard them and heard the old man shouting in English, it must have been poetry, something unclear about being uncertain: "Not what I thought I saw!" Simon returned inside the bookstore and walked between the shelves, his head swiveling for her but she was not on the ground floor nor upstairs nor down. He stood alone without her, within feet of where they'd first spoken, held this unsealed envelope with a name and address that might be hers on the outside. And if the envelope was empty he supposed he'd tear it up and throw it away, but there was something inside and he'd have to see what it was in case it was important and needed to be returned to her.

The envelope contained a personal check and a letter written to Jackie O'Connell. It was a local address and the return address on the envelope was in Connecticut. So it was Jackie he'd talked to and seen. He could, he supposed, take it to her home and put it in the mailbox, or get a fresh envelope and re-mail it himself, but he knew he had to see her again, now that fate had forced this on him. There might be no such thing as fate, but if there was, there was a reason for this envelope to come into his hands. He was meant to know Jackie O'Connell. Fate or coincidence, he would return the envelope in person and see how things went, love or casual sex or nothing at all—he already had the nothing at all, that was all he had to lose.

But if he buzzed her apartment building door, she probably wouldn't let him in and that would be the end of it, he would lose the little Irish beauty again with only her name as additional knowledge. Still, it was all he could imagine to do, he wasn't going to stake her out like a cop or stalk her, he would wait until evening and pray that she liked him enough to let him in, or to come out and see him.

He drank in North Beach with the letter in his back pocket. He hadn't read the letter, he refused to invade her privacy, it would only tell him things he would have to pretend not to know. And he only wanted to know those things she would willingly reveal.

The building was lower Nob Hill, that is, Leavenworth and Post, that is, a dump. He felt better about the odds of her liking him, worse about the odds of her letting him in. There was a chill outside and he wore no jacket, only the drinks inside him. It wasn't that far from home, but he really hoped she let him in, at least for a little while.

Simon found O'Connell, #23, and pressed the buzzer. He wished he had a drink or something. This would be a good time to be someone who smoked.

"Yeah," she answered, and he tried to recognize the voice through the distortion.

"I have your envelope. Your check. My name's Simon. We met in the bookstore."

There was no immediate answer. He waited for the brush-off. But still she said nothing. Simon waited.

"Yeah. Okay."

The door buzzed.

Simon leapt to it, like it was a mistake and he wanted to get in before it was discovered. He pushed the door open and stood with his knees bent for a moment, as though ready to fire with either weapon. But no one was coming, there was no imminent eviction, it was actually a sort of forced invitation and now he had to reply.

Only the second floor anyway, he'd try to take the stairs slowly, to reduce the evidence of his anxiety to see her, but maybe she thought he was taking the elevator. Not that it could outrace him. Simon shook his head, like somehow he could make it clear, like it was a thing he could control. He walked up the stairs, not slowly but as slowly as he could. He wanted her and she was letting him in. He was returning her check and letter, and if she'd wanted him to leave them in her mail she could have said that. Maybe she regretted walking away from him, maybe she was glad she'd dropped that envelope, maybe she was sorry she was no good with pickup lines either.

Simon was nervous, like a high school date. He'd had none of those, but he knew the concept: a total lack of knowledge of the opposite sex, which led to fantasies about their perfection, accompanied by rabid sexual frustration. And he wasn't much past any of that, girls liked him more now because they liked the idea of him as an artist and in high school no one had seen that. He was still shy, still lacked confidence with women, only now it seemed easier for them to see something about him they could like.

Simon stood outside room 23. He pressed the buzzer.

"A sec!" she called from behind the door.

Simon waited. A moment, two. Then the door pulled slowly open as far as the chain on the latch would allow.

"Pass the envelope," hissed the voice.

Simon reached automatically for his back pocket. His hand was on the envelope when the door slid almost shut. Then it opened again. Without the chain this time.

"Hi, Simon," she said, took the letter like a handshake and threw it behind her. "Thanks. Should we get a drink or something?"

Simon looked down at her red hair and her bright blue eyes, both higher up than he expected. She looked up at him and the face was the same, but she was too tall. She had to be five foot eight, at least a hundred thirty pounds.

"You're Jackie?"

"Uh huh."

"Where's your sister?"

Simon stood outside the door, assumed he looked as idiotic as he felt.

"I don't have a sister."

Simon knew he looked dumber than ever. He didn't dare ask, "And we met this afternoon?" or anything like that. But he knew this was not the woman he had seen in the bookstore, this was only someone who looked like her.

"Simon," she said. "Thanks for helping me find the Art section."

The freckles the same, the nose the same. The lips and the hair contrasted as they had this afternoon. But this woman was half a foot taller than the stranger who'd asked him for help. Yet she claimed to be the same person.

"Yeah," he said. "Let's get a drink."

She left the building with him, but they argued at the bar and she stormed off. Simon had not read the script I had written but his deviations from it were minute. Transcripts of the recorded dialogue were nearly identical to the scenes as I planned them. If Simon returned to the apartment building after their one-and-only date she would not be there to let him in, and if he somehow got into the building she would not be in that room. If he truly thought they were sisters he was right, but she would never tell him that, the Jackies worked for me. On a case this big there were plenty of operatives available, the street poet included, and I got to coordinate all of them, every detail of doubt, as they bumped into Parker or mumbled his own uncertain words back at him, the whole world a reminder of the unreliability of his senses.

I got to Parker's neighborhood shortly after dawn and prowled for a parking place. I knew his schedule, he didn't usually get out before nine o'clock, but parking in San Francisco is hard enough without being choosy and I wanted to be as close to his place as possible.

I circled and stopped for an hour, double parked in wait. Later in the day the sidewalks would be littered with hookers, many of them ugly. For now they were littered. And although plenty of the buildings were apartment houses, they weren't the kind that had garages. All the parking along the curb was taken, including the spaces in front of fire hydrants. But even these rundown apartments wouldn't be cheap, most of their residents had to be employed. Someone would have to drive to work soon.

Eventually a slouching young man tumbled around a corner. He looked as weary as his suit, his tie still loose at the collar. He got closer to me and I tensed, hoped he had a car and that it wasn't too small. My Buick had its limits. I smiled as he stepped up to a car as old and American as mine. Thank God for Oldsmobiles. He got in and I took off my emergency brake, my eyes checking for other opportunists while he turned over the time-worn engine. It started on the third try. I backed up a hair, gave him enough room to get out but stayed close enough to the space to maintain my claim. He pulled out and I slammed my way forward then parallel parked before anyone else could get there. I gave the car a comfortable fit, angled so I could get out quickly when I had to. Only then did I open my thermos and pour myself a cup, sipping slowly from my vantage point at the bottom of the block.

It was still early so I got out and stretched my legs, found an alley and pissed, not the sort of crime anyone legislated against. At eight o'clock I took one last good stretch and got back into the car. Now I had to sit and be patient, now the nerves would set in.

A few minutes after ten Parker finally emerged, loped down the stairs three at a time. He moved vigorously, his head bobbing side to side. I slunk down, avoided his flitting gaze. He looked at everything, tried to see something. Not what he was about to see.

I picked up my phone.

"He's leaving now."

Across the street from Parker's building was a deli. He was halfway down the crosswalk when the deli door opened. A man who looked like Otto Workman stepped out.

From my view through the windshield, the effect was

impressive. The Workman ringer was dressed in a suit similar to one worn by Workman in one of his last promo shots. Parker froze in the middle of the street. The double crossed, passed Parker with a smile and a tip of his gray fedora, as Otto would have done if he'd seen he was noticed.

Parker turned to watch the man go. He stood there in the crosswalk, stared as though at a ghost. The light changed but Parker remained, transfixed. Car horns blared and he awakened, staggered back in the direction he'd come.

Parker leaned against his building, looked down the street after the ersatz Workman, now a full block away.

Suddenly he pushed himself off the wall and down the hill, his long strides in pursuit.

I started my car, tried to get out while Parker was still focused, before he caught me with a stray glance. I shouldn't have stayed this long.

I shot out of the parking place and swung a tight U-turn in the wide street, knew I had to get down the hill fast.

Parker might see my car this time, but it would be the only time. I rolled through the stop sign and onto the next block, shouted "Move it!" through an open window as I passed our Workman.

He didn't look my way but he knew it was me, and I knew Parker wouldn't catch him.

Parker had certainly been spooked, but possibly not converted. I considered this over a late morning cheeseburger at Clown Alley. A follow-up would be required. I thought what he'd seen would be enough to keep Parker down, but a professional always kicks to make sure.

The Workman lookalike had been an attempt at dislodging a specific thought. The next move had to go deeper. It was not enough to make Parker uncertain of one fact, for any single idea is susceptible to change. His entire thought process had to become a rudderless boat, at the whim of the wind.

I knew something about Parker now, how his mind worked, how easily he could be swayed. I had fed him ideas from outside himself. The final poisoning would come from within.

He had random meetings with strangers who spouted back at him his own words of doubt, words he had spoken to me. At odd moments someone in mid-conversation would bump into him, leave Simon with sentence fragments: don't know what—I saw—don't know what I did—didn't see anything—didn't know —couldn't tell—I don't know—I don't remember—couldn't see —didn't—couldn't—don't...

I spent the next few days watching, became convinced I'd been right about the kid. He was an open-minded artist, he must have thought he'd had a revelation regarding what he'd seen, a revelation that the only thing he could be sure of was his uncertainty. No longer darting about, he slowed to see what it was he might have missed before. In conversation he stammered and rambled, a charming combination. He would stop in the midst of one of his journeys, stop and stare at something only he could see. And even after the soberest night, his morning eyes were bloodshot.

As a witness he did little for the prosecution's case. Sherilee's attorneys had my reports, which were thorough. He refuted (under cross-examination) his earlier claim that it was Sherilee Malcolm he had seen, or certainly he would have recognized her instantly, not merely in retrospect. Nor could he be sure how soon after the shooting he had seen a woman run down the sidewalk, he may have blacked out, and he certainly never saw anyone get out of the car after the shooting. And whether that woman on the sidewalk had been tall or short or in between, he could not say, although he was pretty certain she did have dark hair. Of course, it was night. Anyway, she was thin, or at least not fat.

Now, three years later, I was again reading Simon Parker's case file. Why had he come back, and what had Hutcheson meant about my carelessness being the cause of his return?

CHAPTER 5
SHERILEE

I COULD NOT BEAR THAT ACQUITTAL, THE IDEA THAT I HAD BEEN tried. As though it could have been me who murdered a man I loved. I know the police like to fall on the spouse or lover as their first suspect, and it can save them a ton of work, but I had no reason to kill Otto. And I would give them none; I gave virtually no answers, relied on my innocence to establish itself. When I was advised that that seemed unlikely to work, I told them to do whatever was necessary, but to keep me out of it.

Even now, four years after the murder and three years after the conclusion of the trial, I do not feel comfortable as Sherilee Malcolm in this city. I need a disguise, and based on the superficial reputation of a well-known writer, it is easy to hide.

My name for now is Sarah Persia, and I will write in the cafés with all the other self-pitying unpublished and unpublishable scriveners, bad poetry on napkins as a signature. It will be alright to say I am an unemployed writer, the city is filled with them, and I can make up my past as I go; I am used to drunken improvising. Perhaps I will establish myself as a new star in this smaller universe. I have received acclaim for my fiction; now I *am* my fiction.

It is a sickness I parade and I know it, this inability to live with who I am, to separate who I am from what I project. All discomforts have become capable of triggering unknown fears, and even the beginnings of sunlight breaking through the fog are enough to alert me to the possibility of a panic attack. And, having wandered into the one section of San Francisco that is frequently sunny while the rest of the city sips endless coffee in its eternal morning haze, I realize that I need this unwanted warmth if I am ever to face my fears.

Still, not every step can be toward discomfort; the heat of the Mission afternoon calls for the removal of my sweatshirt. The T-shirt beneath, from a North Beach movie memorabilia shop, shows Robert Mitchum with "Love" and "Hate" written on his fingers. I fold up my sweatshirt and wedge it into my purse, sip my iced coffee and, notebook open, write about myself, enjoying my anonymity among the living.

For some of the coffee shop crowd I'm too old. This is not news, but an unpleasant reminder, compounded by my ready equating of aging and dying. Yet the young lovers remain sweet to watch, and sometimes they smile back, or at least are smiling when their heads happen to turn my way. I was young once and won't pass for it twice; I know what it means to "look good for your age." Two steps from the glue factory as far as the young colts are concerned.

I've been living as an adult for more than twenty years, and some of them show. Yet I retain fragments of a forsaken adolescence, and when I light a fresh cigarette it's still partly to look cool. I have always posed, only now I think I know when I do it, now I control the situation, I live it.

If I live. Too much of my time seems without purpose except to precede death. Life leads to death as day leads to night, and it is the destination that is important, not the path. I am incapable of imbuing these hours with any meaning, incapable even of witnessing their passing. Thus, the meaningless blur of an afternoon that drags forever yet disappears in an instant, and I am alone somewhere dark, that much closer to where I belong.

"Sarah," I said, with the briefest of glances at the stranger, "and I believe I will have another, thank you."

He looked about my age, the smallest of sun wrinkles beginning beside his eyes, the slightest of squints retained in the shadowed barroom. His brows and hair were blond and thick, the hair of medium length, and his short-sleeved blue shirt was dappled with teardrops of paint stains, as though placed there with the tip of the brush for effect.

I drank rum and coke, allowed my shoulders to slope, and had been concertedly trying to relax since before his arrival. There was a longshot he could help. His hips rolled like he owned this jungle, matter-of-fact, not ostentatious, his gleaming eyes seeking something but not expecting it. He had eased onto the stool beside mine as though he belonged there, and I didn't want to doubt the instincts of such an animal.

His name was Ron, and forgive his appearance, he was a working-class painter, worked all day and, before going out tonight, had a sudden inspiration to add to his current piece.

"Inspiration. I've heard of it."

He smiled, seemingly anxious, and I lit my cigarette rapidly before he could offer. I didn't want to have to refuse him, but I do hate to lean toward anyone I don't know. I smirked at myself —maybe I shouldn't bother trying to relax—and Ron saw the smile coming back at him. I saw his grip loosen on his glass before he raised it to his lips.

And I remembered I intended to meet new people, preferably artists, in this venture, and Ron might even be good, or know someone who was. Regardless, unless he was a moron, it should be worth my time to watch him walk, to observe the predator rightly comfortable in its environment. I smiled anew, and this time it was for him, but he was finishing his drink and did not see. I took a long puff on my death stick, flicked the ashes in the tray, gulped some air, and finished my drink with him.

"What do you paint?" I asked, waiting with Ron for the bartender.

"Oh, this and that, what I see, the same old pretentious shit."

His eyes were fixed on mine, they did not leave. He waited for me to speak.

I lowered my glass without taking a drink. "And what do you see?"

He shrugged. "Usually, something sinister laughing from behind the canvas."

I leaned forward, my brows bearing down. "And is that what you paint?"

"Umm, that's what I can't paint. Although," he added quickly, leaning toward me, "I sometimes catch its lurking shadow."

Not bad, I thought, for bar talk. But let's see how it lasts.

Our faces were too close. I drew mine away. "Reminds me of Flannery O'Connor," I said.

His head tilted back, surprised. He waited. I grinned.

"'The best comedy,'" I quoted, "'shows the skull behind the smile.'"

Ron grinned as well. "I see no skull," he said.

"Comedy's never been my forte."

"Is it safe to suspect you write?"

"It's never safe to suspect anyone of anything."

I took a drink. The conversation was taking a personal tone, and that had not been my intent.

"But you do?" he asked.

"Nothing today, nothing yesterday. Nothing worth mentioning. Notes, scribbles, journal writing. The autobiography of a not very interesting life."

"You don't seem dull to me."

"You want to paint me."

"Probably. But it's better to know you first, to know what there is to paint. To like you or dislike you enough to care what you look like, what you show."

I sipped, and smiled. "I'm trying to hide."

"That could be interesting too. From what or who?"

I shook my head. "From the well-known and the unknown. Nothing I want to talk about. Letting you know it's there, that's all."

"Telling me what you won't tell me? Sounds like you're undecided."

"Maybe I am."

Since Otto's murder I can't write anything that matters. I try but all that comes out is self-pitying garbage. Because I'm overwhelmed by gloom, and a sense of culpability. Because my best friend was murdered and that screwed up my world. And I was accused, and *that* screwed up my world. I've lost my ability to write, to express myself as I am and still find people who love me. I would like to believe this is only a stage of transition, but I'm afraid it's a transition on my way to a permanent Hell.

Now I find myself friendless, almost soulless, and I realize that only through writing fiction do I spend much time telling the truth. I'm consigning myself to doomed relationships, for if one begins to succeed, it won't be the real me who is succeeding but this fictional character I've created.

My old world has ended, I have disappeared from it. I've changed the color of my hair and how I dress, where I live—a choice compelled by the cost of the defense attorneys, successful writer or no—and the people I see. I've embarked on an adventure, but now my life becomes a research project rather than reality. I view myself from the third person.

Physically I no longer appear the same. Emotionally I'm still a wreck, but I think I may be able to deal with the wreckage this way. Yet I also fear I may be jumping from one runaway train to another.

It is Otto who has died, but I who have become a ghost.

His hair was always calling out for combing, it seemed a matter beyond Otto's control. He would run his hand through it, flip it one way or another, but it remained clear that the shambles on his head was a permanent fixture.

Craning his neck and smiling, he was always too busy discovering something to be concerned with his appearance. But the way his clothes were almost right, the way he was clean without being tidy, the frequency with which he would spill a drop from his first cup of coffee onto his otherwise spotless shirt, suggested the at least subconscious desire to look disheveled, that he was more comfortable that way.

The beat writers he admired, and with whom he was sometimes associated, tended to wear suits. I don't think he ever felt at home with them. Or with anyone else, including me. Thus the constant activity, a man at sea because he feared land. He had but one home, and that was on the page, a fictional existence.

A student of many cultures, Otto could not embrace them all, but found their strengths and weaknesses and invested his creations with them, creations not only in his fiction but in aspects of himself. Never fully formed nor did he believe he should have been, he claimed it was the creating and the creations, that to stop was to grow stagnant, that satisfaction-repetition-habits were not merely the lazy route but death before death; he wanted to change but he wanted to initiate the change. That his life was stopped before he was done with it may have saddened his survivors more than it would have Otto, for he had no intention of reaching a point at which his life would have been complete.

If he was murdered by someone he knew, then Otto's greatest sadness would have been in not knowing her as he wished. The anger she felt may have been something he thought necessary to inspire, but the response he received could not have been one he sought. Drama added to his own life was fine, desired, but not if he could not write about it.

I met Ron at a café and he brought a small painting; it was not bad, it was not serene. I did not see that laughing lurker he claims is behind all his work, and I would have if it had been great, I am sure, but he is no idiot, he can put almost into words what it is he seeks and it is something magical, something worth seeking.

I didn't know him well enough to tell him what I thought of it, maybe didn't know art well enough, but I felt I had to speak.

"I wish I could do that," I said. "Show what I see, what I feel. I've been trying to write for so long, I need to get away from words. And I can't do it when I'm alone. There they surround me."

Ron nodded. "With me, it's images. Pictures. Sometimes they fade before I reach the canvas, sometimes after I put them there."

His small painting—an eyeless Raggedy Ann propped against a kitchen table, slumped forward in its chair, gun in misshapen hand, blood cascading from its open skull—was replaced in his briefcase; we returned to the pleasures of coffee and talking around what we meant.

"I don't mind that nothing I write ever comes out as intended. I'm grateful for that. I'm not sure there's enough surprise. Or when there is, have I said anything, or only made something up?"

"I'd like to read something you've written."

"There's nothing worth reading right now. Maybe I'll change my mind. After some time. Maybe then."

Ron tapped a finger on the top of his cup. "Time for what?"

I shrugged, not wanting to be glib, even if I could manage to be clever, which I doubted. Time was what I needed, thought I needed, but I certainly didn't know what it was for.

I am no more than a snake, shedding a skin I wore too long. I had become an aspect of my fiction. In this new fiction, I have allowed myself the possibility of reality, a possibility Sherilee Malcolm no longer had.

Yet I retain her income, she is my means of support, I know no other way. Her agent holds my royalty checks. I do not have the courage to walk naked and be branded insane, I know only the world that everyone else knows, and perhaps my remaining time is to learn how to strip myself. I don't know how to do that except to write, and to write in such a way that this new self rebels against the old and I murder the coddled bitch. I walk now like everyone else walks, none of us reveals anything. I am still a writer who needs something to write. And there I find my skin is not fully shed. Whoever I am, I am not a writer, that is a job I have taken, a calling perhaps, but I do not believe I am spoken to by Gods, only that I am good with words, and I need to make a concerted effort not to write, and see what I become. Is there something inside me that comes out another way, or doesn't need to come out at all? Then what do I do, I do not know, but this above all, I must not write.

CHAPTER 6
WASH

THE GLARE OF LATE AFTERNOON SUNLIGHT SHOT THROUGH THE OPEN window shades behind me as I walked into the bar and tried to find that lanky boy of three years before. But what I faced now was trouble somehow of my own making: a glowering beast, his eyes on me as I edged closer, his every intake of breath a display of unwavering strength. My own breath caught in my throat. I coughed it clear, inhaled deeply. I sat on a stool beside his, nodded and ordered a beer, lay money on the bar. For the feeling of control I had to have while working, a quieting of the nerves would be required.

"Simon," I said in greeting, as casually as I could, wondering what Hutcheson had left out of the file, how Parker had been able to find me.

"Wash," the massive man answered. Even his voice had broadened with the years, become as deep as his shoulders were wide. I was not small, but Parker looked capable of lifting me over his head and hurling me across the room. Didn't look like he'd mind, either.

He said nothing beyond my name. The room was almost empty, and the muted music, cowering from some crevice

51

behind the bar, wasn't nearly distracting enough; it allowed for normal conversation. Parker did nothing but stare.

Reluctantly, I spoke. "You asked to see me. Why?"

Parker looked at me with a sadistic grin, like he'd turned on the lights and found a cockroach at his feet.

"You changed my life," he answered. "You made me see things I wasn't looking for. That doesn't make you right or wrong, it only means you're powerful. I became curious about the source of that power, and contacted your Mr. Hutcheson. Apparently I wasn't supposed to discover his existence."

My change and a glass of draft sat before me. I picked up the latter and gulped.

"How did you find him?" I asked, as casually as I could.

"I saw you on the street one day. You weren't that hard to follow."

"Oh shit. But why?"

With an easy roll of thumb and forefinger, Parker turned the bottle of beer in his hand.

"Of course. I was only a witness, that's how you'd think of it. And the uncertainty you planted in my head was of no consequence to anything but your case. Otto Workman was dead, and there was nothing to be done about it, nothing to do but protect the living. I'd seen your client kill Workman, but that was only an obstacle to you. And when you'd confused me, made me doubt my own eyes, like I panicked and imagined it all, when you had me so fucked up I couldn't believe anything I saw," Parker stopped for a breath and looked me over, "that's when you left me to find my own way."

He paused, as though letting something sink in. "I take it your position of security isn't so critical you'll have to kill me. Buying me off is probably in order."

"You want money?"

"Let's finish these and go somewhere private. I want to talk business."

Chagrined at having been tailed by a fucking art student, I quickly agreed to this suggestion of discretion.

His room was virtually bare, with a couple of folding chairs and a small square table, a stereo in one corner and a television in another.

"Decided I could afford to live alone," Parker explained, "but nowhere nice."

"Where's all the sculptures?"

"In storage. Oh, there's a couple in my room, and one I play with in my spare time, but a friend with a bigger place wanted them for the ambience."

"Christ. Those things are like zombies."

"Yeah, well, he's kind of a death rocker. So I have all this space."

We'd stopped for beer on the way and I pulled a couple out of the bag, set them on the table. "You got an opener?"

"In the kitchen." Parker swooped up the remains of the six pack and in two long steps was out of the room. He returned a minute later, church key in hand. We sat at the little table and Parker leaned back, relaxing as much as he could, crossed his legs and drank his beer, overflowed the meager space the chair provided.

I opened my own beer and leaned back, with less effort than my host. Yet he was the one who was calm. I found myself needing to prompt him.

"So," I asked, "what is this business you need to discuss?"

"The business you do. Your agency. You'll do anything for money, right? Or in this case, for silence."

I shifted in my chair. "What did you have in mind?"

"There's a woman. Don't worry," he grinned. "It's nothing you haven't done before."

In my head, I brushed the back of one hand across my forehead. In reality my back clenched, but I tried to give no tells as I drank some beer. "I usually work witnesses. That's my specialty."

"That's all I ask. I admire your work. After all, I'm a piece of it."

"What do you want me to do?"

The big man smiled again, but he didn't look happy, looked incapable of pleasure. Clearly vengeance, and as much as he could enjoy anything, he was going to enjoy this. A part of me looked on in appreciation of his position, but I knew that whatever Parker had chosen to do I would have to respond, perhaps violently.

"Work a witness, Wash. That's what you do. Maybe you can make him see things. Like you made me see."

Parker drank. I drank too. Prompting him wasn't working; his composure seemed to feed on my impatience. Whatever game we were going to play would be preceded by this one of waiting and drinking. I was willing to hold out as long as the beer did.

I finished my bottle and set it down between us. "Where's the fridge?"

Parker looked up at me with a lazy smile. "Finished already?"

"There's a lot of beer in the world. I wanna make sure I get my share."

Parker kept smiling, didn't tell me a thing, so I stepped quickly into the kitchen.

"You want one?" I called.

"Yeah, sure."

When I returned to the living room, Parker, too, had an empty bottle.

"Not so superior now," I said, handing him his beer.

"Never again," he answered with a yawn and a blink. "You lifted that mask from my eyes."

"Or you think it was me," I said, irritated with the direction the conversation was taking. "But who can say for sure? Maybe it was someone who looked like me."

"Looked like you? No. I'd never met you before that day

years ago. You were no one I'd heard of, and you reminded me of no one."

"I'm touched."

"You don't understand, Wash. The bust of Sherilee Malcolm remains incomplete. By the end of her trial, I was incapable of remembering her face as I'd seen it that night. In that otherwise clear vision her face had become indistinct, blurred. But your face I could remember. It's taken me some time to finish because I keep remembering little things about you, angles of your face you would show only once. And I had to visualize all those angles, and more, the ones you'd hidden from me. But now it's complete. It's in the bedroom. Come."

"You don't get me in the bedroom that easy, sweet stuff. You gotta seduce me first."

"Cut the crap, Shank. I want you to see this."

I sat still, took a drink. "Give me a reason I'd want to."

"Most people would be curious."

"I know what I look like. Don't care if you do too."

With two fingers Parker peeled back a corner of his beer label. His eyes returned to mine. "Maybe you'd like to know how the story ends."

"What story is that?"

"The story you interrupted. The story that was going to be about Otto Workman, and how his friend and sometime lover Sherilee Malcolm killed him, until you intervened with your persuasive powers, causing the only witness to doubt not only his own eyes but himself. How a man died and his killer walked free. How you altered my life with no apparent cost to yourself; how you set free a murderer—"

"Your testimony got her off. And she deserved to get off. You couldn't be sure of what you saw—"

"Because of you!" Parker slammed his clenched fist on the table; it shook. "Everyone has a moment of weakness. You crept around 'til you found mine and you exploited it. I knew what I'd seen."

I drank while Parker spoke, my eyes peering past the bottom of my bottle. When he was finished I shook my head. I spoke more slowly than he had. There was something I had to explain.

"You still don't see. If your weakness could be exploited by something as harmless as words, what could the panic of having seen an actual murder do to it? You were an incompetent witness, Simon. No one with such a weak mind could be trusted as the only witness to a murder. Sherilee Malcolm deserved to walk."

"But I saw her—"

"You don't know what you saw. You were a boy then, remember? You didn't have the confidence you have now."

The forcefulness Parker had briefly flashed was gone, replaced by the uncertainty of a small child lost in an immense body, a scared boy trapped in a room gone suddenly dark. He'd brought me here to play his little game, with righteousness on his side. He hadn't expected me to refuse. Some people never expect the obvious.

I was supposed to have seen his statue of me, and to have reacted in some way, and that, presumably, would have been his revenge. For what I had done to him. But I had done nothing, did not require his judgment. It was not my fault he was a witness. If in his art he saw and showed me with scalding accuracy, it had no bearing on the case.

I couldn't tell from his empty eyes if he was listening. I spoke anyway.

"What about this witness, Simon? This trouble with a woman? Is this something real, or a ploy? Because if it's a real case, I'd like to start on it right away. Get it over with."

"I was the witness before, and you shook my confidence then."

"And now?"

"It's happened again."

I swallowed before responding. "What's happened again?"

Parker swallowed too. "Another murder."

I shook my head. "Who's dead?"

"I don't know. No one I know."

"So what's this got to do with you?"

"The woman down the hall. I swear it's her. I've seen another murder and I swear it's her. Only I don't know."

"You want me to talk to you?"

"I don't know what I've seen. I don't know if I've seen anything. You stopped me from seeing before. Now you have to help me to see again."

"What is it you're not sure about?"

The words rolled out. It wasn't that he wasn't sure if the woman he'd seen commit the murder had actually been the woman down the hall—Alice—he couldn't be sure he'd seen a murder, he was no longer sure he'd gone out that night, walking by that alley he couldn't quite place—and he'd gone walking many times since, searching for it—maybe he'd stayed home and dreamed the whole thing. He'd passed out that night, drinking alone, and he couldn't be sure what happened afterward. Was he unlucky, "always walking into places and seeing these things," or was he cursed from now on to see murders that never happened? Women killers weren't that common he was sure, that is, women *as* killers, and here he'd seen it happen twice. Or at least once. In three years. There was no doubt about the first time, was there?

—No, the first time was definitely a murder.—

And what about now?

—What about now? When had it happened?—

He couldn't be sure, a few days ago, within the week, he hadn't slept well since, he'd lost track of the days. But when he'd gone out if any of it happened all of it happened. He'd talked to police that night, had told them his story, they'd said they'd call him when they needed him. They hadn't called him yet but he didn't know how long it had been, maybe a couple of days.

And he was alone, and the walls could be falling down, he didn't know, the building could be condemned, he didn't care, but the windows looked in on him. He was alone and I saw him there. The words fell from his lips like jettisoned cargo.

He hoped I might somehow save him, but I didn't see what could have made his weakness, a small flaw three years ago, snowball into this force that overwhelmed him now. If it was his own mind I was to save him from, I was out of my league. Yet I was compelled to help, I'd liked the kid, and maybe even felt a little responsible, although the extent of Parker's current difficulties had nothing to do with me.

"I'll try to help you, Simon. Tell me what you saw."

"It was night, I don't know how late. I was home, had a couple beers with friends, then they split and I got drunk. I woke up on the floor and knew I was gonna have a helluva hangover in the morning if I went to sleep, so I got up and drank a couple glasses of water. That wasn't enough to clear my head. I went for a walk."

Parker took two steps away from me, turned and faced me again. He took a long step forward and stood behind his chair.

"It was cold out and I knew it would be, so I put on my heavy coat. It's black, that's why I mention it. When I wear it I blend into the shadows.

"I still do a lot of walking, and I don't remember where I went, so I guess I went a long way, but I was on my way back and probably close to home when I saw the murder this time. I was walking past an alley, and I heard a scream and looked in. There was the woman, turning around, and it looked like Alice —that's the woman down the hall. She had a knife in her hand, and I was feeling sick, and there was a body on the ground behind her. I stepped back, hoped she hadn't seen me, turned and walked the other way. I walked quietly until I reached the corner, then I turned it and ran. I ran home as fast as I could and called the cops."

I got up slowly, needed to take a leak, needed to get away for a minute. When I returned from the bathroom, the last two beers sat open on the table. I reached for mine wearily, drank from it greedily.

"This Alice," I asked, "is she a big woman?"

Parker shrugged. "Average height."

"But is she big? Brawny? Tough looking?"

"Hardly."

"Why didn't you confront her in the alley?"

"She had a knife."

"You could have taken it from her. You're a big man. You could have scared it out of her hand."

"I don't know. I felt sick. I don't know what I could have done."

"So you backed away and ran. Afraid of this little woman with a knife."

"I was sick and she had a knife."

I snorted. "Would you be afraid of me if I had a knife?"

"No." Simon blinked, looked at his bottle then again at me. "I don't think so."

"But this woman, you would. Sounds like you dreamed the whole thing, Simon. A bad drunken nightmare. I don't see you being scared so easy."

"But it could've happened. I was too drunk to think straight. Anything could've happened."

"Maybe you shouldn't get drunk."

Simon glared at me, but the fatigue in his voice left little room for venom. "I want you to talk to Alice. Discreetly."

"Discreetly mentioning the murder she may have committed?"

"I don't care how you do it. But you can't let her know you're working for me. Her last name's House and she lives in number fourteen."

"Well, with that much information, it should be no problem casually bumping into her."

"That's your job. You help me or I go to Hutcheson."

"Don't bother. Now that Hutcheson knows who you are, he'll be keeping an eye on you."

I promised I'd look into things for him, then finished my beer fast, left Parker and his new quiet room.

Outside the night was black and there were no streetlights, only stars and the light escaping from buildings. I had to walk a few dark blocks before I reached my car, and I passed some alleys along the way, but no one was being murdered in any of them, not at the moment. Each one seemed a likely place for leaving someone behind.

I found my car and drove home but had nothing to do when I got there, it was too early for sleep. The talk with Parker had done nothing to relax me. I tried thinking about it, but my thoughts did not change or become clearer; they lay stagnant in my mind like muck at the top of a pool. I sat on the edge of the bed, my elbows on my knees, still dressed except for my bare feet. I put my socks back on, then my tennis shoes. I wanted to have a clear head in the morning, but first I had to make it through the night, and all I could think was I should take a walk.

CHAPTER 7
SHERILEE

Unplanned morning I grabbed T-shirt, sweater, and jeans, realized I was dressing like a folk singer, and looked for my favorite cheap necklace, a plastic blue beaded Mardi Gras job. I'd worn it a few days earlier, but that was before I moved, so I gave up quickly when it wasn't in its drawer and went out my natural hair color away from looking far too much like that of Joan Baez. Ah well, folkies do come a lot uglier.

And I know better than to take seriously my preoccupation with superficial appearance, but living in disguise alerts me to my camouflage.

This morning's coffee would, as usual, be drunk alone in public. Ron worked too early for any weekday breakfasts; perhaps a lunch someday, he'd said.

"If it's romance you're after," I'd answered, "I'm afraid you'll have to wait."

"It's the unknown I'm after."

I'd nodded. He wasn't someone to be rapidly deserted. There was a distinct possibility he really gave a shit. For now, we ate no more than pastries together, something the coffee would wash down, and we sat at our tables in often silent immersion. I liked the way stray hairs would jut out from behind his ears in bunches like sideways tail feathers, I liked the shape of his chest under his shirt, I liked the way his Adam's apple moved when he swallowed.

His head would bob earnestly when I spoke, he would hesitate ever so slightly before answering. Nothing rehearsed, absorbing my words before responding. He could be clever, but was not at my expense, that is, not at the expense of my thoughts. Of course, we'd met three times, and men are always sweeter before you get to know them. Spider and the fly.

There was only one café close enough for my first coffee, and almost always I plopped into the nearest chair as soon as I got my cup. Yet, tired as I was this morning, when the familiar face behind the counter greeted me with, "Large coffee?" I realized the rut I was already in and quickly added, "to go."

Tried to walk out of this new habit but slowly, down the street, sipped, not knowing where I would go. Where I could go, where there was to go.

The silence in conversations with Ron: the mutual observation of facial expressions, although a dialogue of its own, is only a prelude to the time when words will flow. This pre-verbal stage we reach is an exercise, the removal of superfluous words, preceding discovery of the words we need.

It's taken me three years to find someone to talk with. I shouldn't be good at it yet. I often talk because I want to talk, but rarely do I talk to someone because I want to talk to that person. The people I listen to are rarely the people I want to talk to. I am compelled to listen when people talk, and to respond to them, to keep the conversation going. But much of this is to immerse myself in their world, to become human like them.

In silence I walked, not in truth, not in anything precious, only a lone woman on an empty, dirty sidewalk. With no destination in mind, not even the place I stopped would be my destination, destiny a distant theory. Discovery is the process I must return to, not this always digging deeper into the same hole.

There were no cars. I stepped into the middle of the street and walked down the vacant, cracked asphalt.

Paparazzi don't chase writers, thus it is easy for me, with my public image limited to the stark visages of author photos, to travel incognito. I have never done it for so long before, I have never had so much to hide from. And there were photographs taken at the trial, but people won't remember those, they can't. It's been three years since that thing ended, since all of this should have ended. I have never felt so abandoned. The blinding light of day is not filtered out by clouds. The darkness of night is no longer an ally.

Nightfall brought death to Otto, was sudden and crushing. That witness at the trial, I could not understand him, saying that when he knew Otto was dead he could hear nothing. I could hear everything. Every word he'd ever said, every sound the city made. Rushing water in screeching pipes, roaring buses and fuming pedestrians left standing, countless sirens and a single pistol shot, I've lost the order of things.

"Father, I want to kill you. Mother, I want to uhhhhhhh!"—Jim Morrison.

Funny boy. At his best at his least articulate. That was when he had the most to say, when he became the animal within, no more mister artsy-fartsy filmmaker-poet, no more bothering with the constraints of a pop band, but leaping into the cacophony, becoming the cacophony, yet remaining human, an asshole even, screaming roaring and singing and doing those things beautifully, dancing and crawling with no view of the absurdity of his appearance, in the context there became nothing absurd about it, but was this only an act? Had he become what no reasonable man would want to be, was this a part of him, or was this something he could do and he did it? And would any of it have been possible without the intervention of chemicals, was any of it anything but artificial? Had his mind been freed, or corrupted?

Cars honked as I made my way down the middle of the road, arms held out for balance. The street was not busy, but I was where I was not supposed to be. The idea of being hit crossed my mind only briefly, I felt no danger, thus not the exhilaration of same. This was a feeling of being afloat, above the world. I was not owned, by others or self, by mind or body.

The viewer of an act associated with insanity may well expect continued and progressively accelerated acts of insanity. If the suspected is innocent—innocent of what? Insanity is not a crime but an illness, thus a drain on society but one for which no one is culpable, yet the perpetrator is to be locked up; thus, in the eyes of society, the sick are as bad as the criminal—or worse, for they will never pay for what they have done, they are never officially blamed—from this viewpoint, if the suspected is innocent (although eccentric, which is distraction enough), then the viewer's knowledge of insanity may place the viewer in something resembling an insane state, anticipating what the "nut" will do next. Like a weak body, a weak mind is more susceptible to illness than is a strong one; the unfortunate surprise is for the mind that inaccurately thought itself strong. For how is a weak mind to know it is weak?

So I rambled down the middle of the street unafraid of cars, knowing I would not walk into them and they would be afraid to drive into me. My insanity only an act, I crossed over to the sidewalk when there were no cars coming, before I reached a busier part of town. It had been a brief straddling of a little white line, a small indulgence, a reminder that those who live on the edge of the cliff do not fear falling but avoid it.

Exhilaration had gone on long enough, had drained me of my artificial strength. It was time for another cup of coffee.

The café I entered was one I had not entered before, the boy behind the counter a complete stranger to me.

"Large coffee," I said, "for here."

I had not waited for his polite greeting, could not allow myself to be fettered by petty resentment if he had neglected me. I frowned on my attitude but knew I always felt snotty in those places where I spent money, expecting polite and friendly acts performed in my direction in exchange for my patronage. It may have been the guilt I felt regarding my treatment of those who served me that caused my usual kindly manner in restaurants and stores, but for the moment I knew my reasons, and the glare intended for myself projected outward. The boy pouring my coffee responded with a smile, gentle and comforting. I wondered if he pitied me, wondered if he saw through me, but saw only concern in his eyes.

"Thank you," I said, paid him, and left an extra dollar on the counter. This was money given freely, in gratitude and without stigma. The debt had not been monetary, but I could not think how else to return the favor.

"You're welcome," he answered, one foot stepping back, his hands balanced against the counter, not lifting the bill.

I smiled, first at the money then at the boy and, not wanting our exchange to degenerate into politeness, I lifted my cup in salute and walked away, looked for a place to sit.

I sat at a table, small and round, made of cheap lightweight metal, with matching chairs, my back to the counter. Customers sat at many of the tables, but most drank coffee of some sort and I wondered how the café remained in business. Behind the counter the boy was busy, his face no longer grinned. Perhaps he could not smile on demand, perhaps he had the wrong job. But of course he did, this was not the sort of work for which anyone would want to be suited. It was a temporary position, something vaguely tolerable prior to something better. Or even something worse, but something less a rut.

His face had been cleanly shaven, not today, but recently; there was not enough stubble to be fashionable. The long cheek-bones reminded me of my own, but younger, kinder. He probably did not know as much of the world as I had at his age; at any rate, life had not hardened him as it had me.

I returned my attention to my coffee and beyond the empty chair before me to the far wall and the row of large paintings that adorned it. Some were dark, some bright, some a combination, but none held my attention. I sat too far away to judge them, close enough to not want to. I saw nothing better to do than to rise and approach, to assure myself I was not mistaken, as I was sure I would not be. The problem with my initial judgments is they are so often correct that I rarely question them, and when I am wrong about something or someone I may remain that way a long time.

I stood before colors swirling in incoherent discord and asked myself why, what was the painter thinking or feeling? The confused clutter looked too much like thought, emotionlessly pummeling the canvas. It is not that I am opposed to experimental art, only that experiments often fail. I looked straight ahead but no longer saw the painting before me, remembered instead the reproduction of a Jackson Pollock painting on an Ornette Coleman album, reassured myself that I was not lost to what was modern, even if the modernism I remembered was thirty years old, for it still offered more that was new than that before me now.

And what was it Pollock and Coleman had offered? The charge through horror, differing from traditional art not in the force of its impact but in its lack of lucidity, not incoherence but the revealing of a feeling without an explanation of that feeling's causes. Sustained communication of such a vision requires a different kind of knowledge, the sharing of a context previously unexpressed. Its aspirations do not necessarily differ from those of traditional artists, only its form. That is, they still show beauty or ugliness, from an angle previously unused, as though looking down from a rock that had remained invisible until it was climbed.

Briefly I looked at each painting on the wall, but none stirred me, none so much as slowed my coffee intake. Not that this painter showed no promise, only that I saw none I wished him to keep.

I finished my cup, flipped it in the air end over end, spun around and snatched it by the handle with extended index finger, returned it to my table with a bow, and sauntered out the door to a small round of applause.

CHAPTER 8
WASH

THE AGENCY DOSSIER ON ALICE HOUSE WAS THIN, CONSISTING primarily of conventional sources—DMV, police records— revealing only conventional information. It was nothing I could use. I already had her name and address, and her old speeding tickets didn't interest me. What did interest me was her photo. Thirty-three and divorced, five foot six and thin, that could apply to anyone. But her face: Alice House was a dead ringer for Sherilee Malcolm. The same pale skin, the same aquiline nose, the same relaxed little lips, as if she were about to speak. It reminded me of a book cover, a cover I'd occasionally looked at long after I'd finished the book. And I thought I'd like to meet this Alice House.

It was a solid guess that no one with the agency would be helping on this case, but Hutcheson hadn't quite said, that so I asked for an operative to help shadow the woman. The tone of Hutcheson's refusal implied I was in trouble even if I got out of this jam, and I regretted asking before I'd hung up the phone.

Parker had given me a copy of his key to the building, and after a quick run up the stairs and an unanswered knock, I opened the door to number fourteen almost as easily, a credit card and in.

In shape her apartment was similar to Parker's, but the decor was more feminine, less spartan. The light blue floor-length curtains had been left open to warm the room with sun and, with the door shut quietly behind me, I blinked rapidly before opting to squint.

The walls had been painted turquoise, and on one hung a large poster of Jimi Hendrix: eyes closed, mouth open, head to the sky. Twin two-seater couches met a small table at right angles, both couches facing the color television in the opposite corner. Under the Hendrix poster was a five-drawer cedar dresser with chipped corners and scratches on the sides and front, like it had been dropped down a flight of stairs. It was four feet high and three feet wide, and on the floor beside it was a large portable cassette deck. None of that interested me, nor did the potted flowers on the window sill. My concern was that the room contained no wastebasket.

Into the kitchen I strode, and under the sink I found it: trash. One bag of nothing but empty diet soda cans, the other more what I was looking for. I removed the newspaper still rolled up in my coat pocket and opened it wide on the floor. Then I went through Alice House's garbage, laid it on the paper. A coffee filter and a Styrofoam ramen cup, a crumpled candy wrapper and a wadded up Kleenex. Cigarette ashes. More coffee filters, a cereal box, a Safeway package that had once contained chicken legs. Nothing dramatic. No syringes, no letters from friends mentioning the murder she'd committed, nothing but kitchen junk. Carefully I returned the garbage to its bag and swept up after myself, left no trace.

The bathroom wastebasket was no better, telling me nothing I didn't already know. The medicine cabinet was filled with cosmetics and lotions, a tube of toothpaste, a box of Q-Tips, various aspirins and medicines. I looked at every little container, pulled the notebook from my pocket and wrote down the names of her drugs, but they all looked like minor painkillers or tension relievers.

Well, there had to be a bedroom and there had to be something in it, and if none of it was incriminating so much the better. When it came right down to it, the more obviously Alice was innocent the easier it would be to tell Parker to forget it, he'd had a bad drunken dream. Despite the haunting resemblance to Sherilee Malcolm.

A door in the living room opened into the bedroom, a small room containing a single bed along the near wall and a dresser opposite. Above the dresser was a painting, a landscape at evening. The sky was light blue, the grass light green, the sun going down. Yet it was oddly dark. The quiet picture reminded me of something, reminded me of faces I hadn't seen in years. I stepped closer, to study it more carefully. There, in the lower right corner, was the signature: S. Parker. Had he given her the painting or had she gotten it some other way? How close had they been, and how recently?

A small bookshelf stood in one corner. I read the titles: *Naked Lunch, Our Lady of the Flowers, On The Road*. Intro to Bohemia 1, I smirked. There were also books by Shirley Jackson, William Faulkner, Richard Wright, Malcolm X. Books on voodoo, tattooing, body modification. Beckett, Shakespeare, Sylvia Plath. Henry James, William James, Emily Brontë, Mary Shelley. Books on Buddhism, books on the sex industry. And filling half of one shelf, a dozen books by Sherilee Malcolm, probably everything she'd written. On the whole I found it charming. Except for that quiet sunset on the wall, casting its evening shadows.

The dresser contained nothing but clothing—skimpy underwear and thick socks—and jewelry. There were photographs on the bedside table, Alice with people who looked something like her. The table had a small drawer, which I opened. Like in a motel, there was a Bible inside. I flipped through it but nothing fell out. A writing tablet lay beneath the book.

There were words on the tablet's pages, words about hating her job, words about hating being alone, wondering if she was any damn good, words about hating the way guys came on to her and words about wanting to live somewhere better. There were no words about a murder, no words about Simon Parker, only a paragraph of complaints on each of two consecutive pages. The remaining pages were blank. I returned the tablet to its place beneath the Bible and hurriedly looked through Alice's closet. All I saw were clothes: boring little spring dresses for work and scantier, trashier dresses for play, a few coats and a passel of shoes similarly mismatched, ranging from the drab little things that passed for fashionable in the financial district to black stiletto heels and a pair of knee-high snakeskin boots. I smiled, shut the closet door, and left the room.

I hadn't bothered to look through the living room bureau and figured I might as well before I left. The top drawer was a mess of receipts and paycheck stubs, coupons and magazines. The other drawers held more magazines and some paperback books, a lot of sloppily folded clothes—the ones she never wore, I guessed—and cassettes; nothing that clashed with what I'd already seen. I shut the drawers, retraced my steps, made sure I was leaving everything as I'd found it, and left Alice House's apartment.

Wanting to talk to Parker, I knocked on his door, but no one answered. I hadn't expected him to be home, only hoped. I walked down the corridor. Tired from the uneventful morning and the long night before, I took the rickety old elevator down to the lobby and walked out of the building. I stood on the sidewalk a moment, undecided, let the summer wind blow across my face, then, no destination in mind, turned to the right and walked down the street.

Parker's studio at the Institute, a black-curtained room: a candle, its wick severely diminished, almost to the point of nonexistence.

All the light in the room provided by the candle's wisp of fire, I tried to find Simon Parker's broad frame. I stood inside the doorway, the weak light from the hall behind me making no discernible dent in the black before me.

"Simon?" I asked the dark. "Are you in here?"

"I'm busy. Can it wait?"

"It's Wash Shank. It's about Alice."

"I know who it is. Can it wait?"

"It's important. Is there a light in here?"

"Fuck. Yeah."

I heard movement, then an overhead light was on, one small bulb shining, sixty watts at the most. In the center of the small square room was a ten-foot-long rectangular table that reached within three feet of two of the walls. The candle, still burning, sat in the center of the table. Around it were square glass boxes, two-inch sides on the smallest, ten inch on the largest.

"What are you doing here? And why in the dark?"

Parker wiped a long sleeve beneath his nose. Disdain settled like dust.

"I'm playing with light and color. It's an experiment. Darkness is a control."

I ignored the irritation in his response. I was curious. "What do the glass boxes do?"

"They reflect light, of course." There was a switch on the table, like the switch on an electric train set. Parker threw it and the boxes moved, each rotating while simultaneously circling the candle.

Parker smiled. "They're orbiting."

"You do that by radio control?"

"Yeah, that's not so hard. Except they crash into each other now and then. A friend of mine helped with the wiring, and when something goes wrong it can take a while to straighten out."

"But what does it do with light and color? Besides reflect the light."

"So far, very little. I've about got the orbit mastered. But in the dark, when I play with the color of the glass, with any luck we get a light show."

"With all the light from a candle?"

"That's the idea. The trick is to make it small enough it's practical. May I turn the light back off?"

I shook my head. "I'm in the dark as is. I'd like to ask some questions."

Parker pulled back the switch and the boxes stopped. "Such as?"

"Such as how well do you know Alice House?"

"We've met, we've talked." Parker sat expressionless, his hands in his lap.

I sat down across from him, Parker's magic light table between us. "Were you ever lovers?"

"What do you know, Wash?"

"I'd like to know if you and Alice were ever lovers."

"Do you know her? Have you asked her?"

"I was hoping I could find out without being that indiscreet."

"What have you found out? What have you done?"

"You asked me to check on Alice House. I'd like to know a little more about her before I meet her. I'd like to know why one of your paintings is in her bedroom."

"What were you doing in her bedroom?"

"Research. What's your painting doing there?"

"She wanted it."

I stood, leaned toward Parker, my fists pressed against the table.

"Is she your girlfriend or what? Tell me everything or I'm quitting your case, and we'll settle this little security leak some other way."

As big as he was, Parker should not have been intimidated. Maybe the bulk was too recent an acquisition for him to think of it as a part of himself. Anyway, he didn't deck me, I doubt the thought crossed his mind. He looked up at me, small and young.

"We went out a few times. We decided—she decided—we were better off as friends. She said I was too moody, too angry. She said she liked the quiet part of me better. So I gave her that painting. So she'd think of me that way."

I'd thought the painting dark, but—"You said she wanted it."

"She did, after I told her she could have it."

I unclenched my fists, stretched my fingers against the edge of the table until some knuckles cracked. "She hadn't seen it before?"

"It was in storage."

"At your friend's house?"

"Yeah, but he kept it away from the sculptures."

Parker looked too relaxed. My palms again balled up into fists.

"You got it out of storage specifically to give to Alice?"

"Yeah."

"Knowing you were breaking up?"

"To show her we could still be friends."

"How long ago was this?"

He looked at the blocks, barely paid me enough attention to answer. "A few months," he said without looking up.

There was no keeping the edge out of my voice. "And you still want her back?"

"I still like her."

"Even though you saw her commit a murder."

Now he looked up. "But I don't know that. I can't be sure."

"But you thought it. And when you thought it, did you still love her?"

Parker shook his head. "I never said I loved her."

"Do you give away your artwork often?"

"No. But like I said, I liked her. I still like her." He was talking to the blocks again.

"I don't want to argue the semantics of the thing. I want an idea of how you feel about her. How you felt. Strongly: is that safe to say?"

"Yeah, sure. So what?"

"So you don't want me to go for the kill finding out about her, do you? You want the truth, so long as it's easy. You want me to get information from her without fucking with her head, you want me to be so subtle she'll give me answers without even hearing the questions."

"That would be ideal—"

"You don't want me to do to her what I did to you, is that it? Or do you? Am I supposed to avenge you for something she did to you, or is it that you don't trust her anymore?"

Parker's eyes shot suddenly at mine. "No. That's stupid. I don't want you to hurt Alice."

My hand tapped the table. "So do you really believe this cock 'n' bull story about seeing her commit a murder, or is there something else you're trying to find out?"

He still looked at me. I had his attention.

"Like what?" he asked, softly.

"Like who she sees, what she does with her spare time. What it is she prefers to you."

"I want to know about the murder. I want to know if I'm going crazy."

"Alice may be able to tell you that, without my help. Your mood swings—do they usually happen when you drink?"

"Maybe sometimes drinking gets me in trouble but some-times there's nothing else I can do. I have to have a good time, I have to relax, and sometimes to do that I have to get out of my head."

"Turn off the light and play with your candle. I have to get back to work."

I still didn't know how to approach Alice House. The meeting with Parker had done nothing to convince me that talking to her would do any good. Parker's motives were too confused, as if either the woman was innocent of murder and their love could be rekindled, or she was guilty and he had been wrong about her all along. No matter. Whatever Parker thought, my reasons for meeting Alice were strictly personal.

Facially, of course, she greatly resembled Sherilee Malcolm, whose gaunt, high cheekbones had last been seen in our city shortly after her acquittal. And the way Alice wore her hair—straight, black, thin, and stopping at the shoulders—the effect had to be intentional.

Sherilee was thirty-two at the time of Workman's murder, and her face was plastered across the papers, a closeup of the book cover from *A Woman's Place Is in Your Face*, with one eye winking and an unlit cigarette caught between lips painted black, her head leaning slightly forward for a light. She was a bad girl grown up poetic, a part of the neo-beat scene and associated with several women's rights groups, groups she didn't need to join to be a part of.

> *Pissing out a window*
> *Now there's an example*
> *Of something a man can do*
> *That a woman wouldn't.*

Malcolm's work was filled with arrogance; she was always out to impress or intimidate, and she often succeeded. Some critics suggested her work lacked tenderness. Sherilee responded that the critics lacked balls.

> *The love I seek is all-consuming, and any woman or man protecting a soft spot had best take leave of my love's domain. Nothing that matters can be held back, whether you want to hold it or not.*

At some point Sherilee and Otto became lovers. It was an affair that continued intermittently until Otto's death.

Death, of course, was where I came in. I never met the accused, but I knew who she was, had enjoyed her early novels. And Workman, the man she may have killed, was, though not much older than me, one of my first heroes. A man of integrity, a man who knew what he believed and could put it into words. That was never a thing I could do, I didn't know what I wanted, much less how to fight for it. I only knew I had to fight. Without a cause, I clung to doing my best. I suppose not having answers should have made me ask questions. What good are heroes if you don't try to be like them? But Otto Workman was like a successful cousin I could admire and that was it. I could never be like him, nothing I could do would ever make me admired.

So I worked with little things, like one man's delusions, and I tried to not only find the truth but to convince him of it. And sometimes I did it with lies, but lies can educate if you tell them right. And maybe that's as close as I come to being like Otto Workman. He told his version of the truth by making up stories. Sometimes I make up stories too, and sometimes they convince a witness of the truth—he's a lousy witness. That's what I'd done with Simon before, but I didn't know what I'd do with him now. I'd convinced him of his uncertainty before, but this time he was already uncertain of what he'd seen. And he had faith in his uncertainty.

I had faith in nothing—I had beliefs not values—and thinking about Otto Workman reminded me of an idealism I'd admired but could never have. My own life had become about my ability to implement tools of doubt, doubt not in human abilities but in humanity. It was hard to say what I got out of this, hard to say what I wanted. I was good at what I did because I believed in it, because I knew that losing faith in yourself is how to see the real world. It was not that I reveled in doubt, or saw beauty in its honesty, but I believed in it, not like people believe in God but like people believe in dust. It is something I accept, not a cause, not a thing to fight for. I don't have a direction, there's nothing I know how to choose. And now I don't know if I idolize Otto Workman anymore; I envy him. He wrote about people who made decisions, and even if those decisions were wrong they acted on them. And that was what made them alive.

CHAPTER 9
SHERILEE/SARAH

As Sarah Persia I am less uncomfortable in a bookstore, less wary of being recognized. Of course, this was the first one I had been in since my return to San Francisco. Finding two used Sherilee Malcolm paperbacks on the shelves, I glanced at the pictures on the back covers, sneered and put them back. Bad photographs apparently are the best promotion, for the books had sold well, although there had been whispers from friends that my writing had something to do with that.

I didn't know what I was looking for, didn't know what I hadn't read that I wanted to read. Something about discovery, something that hadn't been written. Which meant I was itching to write again, but I was not inspired, I had no ideas. I sought writing so great it would lift me, that feeling of possession, of loss of self, that occurs within the pages of a great book. The nightmares that stopped me from finishing *Crime and Punishment* the first time I tried to read it, the realization that I was inside someone else, taken captive. The fiction shelves were too vast, my eyes blurred, the poetry shelves too meager. I glanced at a couple of volumes but nothing held me hostage and that was how I needed to be held. There were the history books, the psychology and philosophy, but I sweated already, I couldn't be seen like this. I had to get back outside where the sweltering sun might give physical cause for my reaction. Feeling drenched in loose jeans and T-shirt I hurried to the door, ran the last several steps. Outside at last. The sun was not what I wanted, but standing in it I felt relieved, I had made my escape.

I took rapid steps onto a section of 16th Street overflowing with bars, stepped inside the first one I got close to—the sign read "Doctor B's,"_and medication was definitely called for—downed a double shot of Glenlivet and ordered a beer, only then noted the bartender's face. My empty hands tensed. Inside my purse, I found a handkerchief and wiped my brow dry.

"Getting hot out there?" she asked.

Beneath dark hair in a page boy cut the dark-complexioned face was almost round, softening its sharp features; below the thin black brows gleamed dark deep-set eyes.

"That ain't the half of it." I paid for my beer and took a deep breath. When she lingered, I winked. "I saw someone out of my past. Someone I thought of as dead. Not that I want her that way, but..."

The bartender nodded. "I know. Seems like the more I want to avoid someone, the more likely I won't."

It was early afternoon and I was the only customer.

"My name's Sarah."

"I'm Christine. Hang on, I just opened. Let me put on some music."

She walked down the bar and into a translucently curtained small room beyond. She walked easily, no force to it, but she swung as though the music had already begun, lightly, and I knew she raked in the tip money. The music she played was some old rhythm and blues vocal group, the singer familiar but no one I could name. Christine strolled back toward me and I smiled broadly, my pansexuality leaning definitely her way.

"This is great," I said, referring to the music, looking at her proud feminine face, large eyes not fully opened, as though not completely awake, yet still shining past her strong, wide nose, and I forced my own eyes away, avoided the temptation to stare, and instead took this moment to look at her lips, not collagen-thick but not too thin. I glanced down at my bottle. "Who is it?"

"Billy Ward and the Dominoes. I bought it."

Christine poured herself a drink and sat on a stool behind the bar. "When my only customer sits down this end," she said, "I have no view of outside. I can't see anything."

"I could move over a little."

Christine shook her head. "I didn't mean it like that. I like it this way."

I blinked, twice.

"I know what's outside," she continued. "Someone in here is better than all the no ones out there."

San Francisco, I thought, you're my kind of town. I sipped my Dos Equis.

The smile had clinched it, as though clinching had been necessary. But she was probably ten years younger than I was, and she might not even like women. Anyway, I needed friends *and* lovers, certainly more of the former.

I knew nothing of her except grace and beauty, and those were enough that I had to give Christine a chance. I would try the friendship angle first, of course. The odds were better. And if that didn't pan out, a friendly bartender walking distance from home was nothing to be scoffed at. Even though it was early on a weekday, I was surprised at the emptiness of the joint.

"I'd expect," I said, "this place to be flooded with men."

Christine shrugged. "We get a later crowd."

"Still," I said, trying to keep my eyes casually on her face, "I'd think you'd pull 'em in."

Christine smiled. "Men in bars. They go for different things. Mostly they come in here to drink." She shrugged again. "Once a place gets a rep…"

"So this is a watering hole?"

"The regulars know who's here."

"Damn." I meant it. Whatever happened to word of mouth? Or maybe it was the unavailability of the bartender, but I thought men liked impossible dreams.

"I love Beckett," I said, "but I don't know if I can write like that."

"What?"

"The distance of people, of language. An inability to communicate. The men who come in here and want you but can't say a word. I guess that's what I was thinking." I took a drink. "Anyway, somewhere in my head it clicked."

"I wish more things would in mine."

Her fingers, curved around the wine glass, were long and lean, the nails short and faintly red. The loose black blouse was buttoned too high for its V-neck to do anything but promise hidden treasures.

———

There were no lapses in our conversation, our silences filled with thought. I had not lost faith in language; that was not why, since Otto's death, I used fewer words. What I had lost was control. Use of a word implied its importance, and the user of unimportant words was unlikely to see the difference.

I could sit and admire and allow my mind to drift, but if it drifted too far I might speak words that would betray me, and any position I had gained might be lost.

Two hours later we were no longer alone, but we may as well have been. The place remained nearly empty, and those who had joined us had not interrupted. But another round and the impression I'd make would not be one I chose.

I thanked Christine for my drinks, and she thanked me for my time. Joyously I turned my back on her, anticipated my return.

"My name is Sarah," I said to the stranger, who replied by telling me a name that may have been his. Since I lied, why not everyone else? Anyway, I was drunk, and tried to remember if I'd worn a ring today. It certainly wasn't on me now.

My other adornments remained, all of them false, as all were a part of this Sarah, but I didn't know how much of anyone else was disguise. I assumed it began with the obvious. False names and false faces.

I sat at a table of babbling strangers and removed my feet from my shoes. The droning went on. About what, I did not know. Or care. It was bullshit, and I could not tell them it was bullshit, they would not have believed words not their own. I felt suffocated into silence. Under the table, I unsnapped the top button of my jeans.

I would not go through with it, I was sure, I was too vain to reveal myself, any piece that was nothing but me. So I drank, one hand remaining under the table, and with all the dexterity in my fingers unsnapped that second button.

There were too many men here, and how would they react? But I hated caring, and I hated being afraid, and I knew I would get out of it somehow, that if I was strong enough to do it I'd be strong enough to walk away.

It wasn't yet cold when I'd come in, I was dressed the same as at noon, T-shirt and jeans and nothing underneath. The dialogue like a swarm of flies buzzed about the table, and I knew what that made me.

The shirt came off first, both arms straight up, then I yanked it off and flung it as I stood and pushed my pants halfway down my thighs. There were gasps and turned heads as I pushed the jeans further, and the noxious dialogue stopped long enough for me to smile.

Then someone was on me, but offering neither pleasure nor pain, only a coat. I flailed, swatted it away, but strong arms forced it around me and a crowd pressed against me, strange hands pulled my pants back up, strange fingers alarmingly close to be doing nothing but snapping buttons back together, the coat replaced by my now retrieved T-shirt.

"No!" I shouted, but a chorus of other idiocies drowned me out, I was escorted outside, and a trio from my table stood with me, silent until the cab arrived.

They opened the door and pushed me in. Barefoot, I rode home.

I wake up in bed fully dressed and sweating, my heart beating I am sure far too fast, the lyric "and these days hearts are cheap" embedded in my brain.

I fumble with my pants, struggle to remove them, wonder where all this heat comes from, it's never this hot in the city. The buttons will not unsnap, my fingers as though swollen unable to move deftly as they should. I stop what I am doing to see if these leaden, lumpy digits can cross each other, and I cannot do it. The buttons remain in their holes. I lie there with my pants still on, my sweat-soaked shirt fastened to my chest.

My heart, I cannot actually feel it accelerating, but I'm sure that it does. This is my body and there is something wrong with it, I cannot say what, I cannot know, only that it is out of balance, it is not in my control. The sweat runs rivers down my arms and forehead. I never sweat.

I lie awake wanting nothing but to be naked, and I cannot undress. I am stuck. I begin to cry, not quietly and increasingly louder. The water coming out of me is a flood. I want only to be naked. I sweat, I cry, I cannot stop. Fumbling fingers meet again at the top of my pants, try once more to unsnap a button, a simple fucking button. I shake, I roar, I cannot do this simple thing, this only thing. I take a deep breath, my lungs are full.

Without stopping the tears, I scream.

They knocked at my door but I wouldn't let them in. I was alone in this, and alone had to remain.

"Go away!" I shouted. "It was a dream!"

I knew they did not believe me. I knew they did not go away, even after they had stopped with their questions, even when there were no more murmurs. I knew they remained outside my door. I did not know how long they would stay there, but I knew they would never be any help, I would never let them in.

I hoped I would not lose the room. It was a nice room. In a nice neighborhood. And I did not mind not knowing the others in the house, except now I wondered what they thought of me. It did not matter. It had never mattered, but for a time I had forgotten.

It was dark, I was alone, that was how it had always been. I did not need them, nor they me. Yet there were others I sought. Perhaps Ron and Christine. Definitely Otto, but how? To be one with his ghost without being dead.

I realized my sweating had stopped.

"Go away," I said softly to the silence behind the door.

I stood, removed my clinging clothes, casually—it was as though they fell off—and, finding the room slightly chilly this way, returned to bed, pulled a blanket over my body, and went to sleep.

But I do not sleep. I know that as a writer I am always trying to finish scenes, but they don't always end so much as drag on until they peter out. I am attempting to structure life, and that is a lie. To lie well, that is art, I know someone's said that, but it means nothing to me now. I am like Alice down the rabbit hole, before she touches bottom, not knowing if she will ever touch bottom, reaching out to grab whatever protrudes from the walls I fall endlessly past. But they are empty shelves, and the fall is incomplete, it may be all I ever do.

Unable to sleep or to rise, I reach up and pull the curtains open a crack to peek out at the darkness, to catch glimpses of the rising sun, in hopes that I will rise with it, or that it will put me to sleep. Anything. But it does not rise. I lie awake. And wait, though I don't know what for.

The fatigue I feel should be enough to let me rest, but I do not. I lie awake, blinking, and I can feel the wetness in my eyes, as though there remain uncried tears. But I do not cry them, I have done enough crying for now, I am tired, I let them sit on my eyes, I do not wipe them away. That is their place, and this is mine.

Murder. MURDER.

CHAPTER 10
WASH

THE FACE HAS NOT YET BEEN FORMED, OR HAS BEEN FORMED AND flattened, voided, the clay pushed and mixed back together, no features revealed, only a narrow shape. This was the sculpture Parker was playing with, the one he couldn't finish. I stood alone in his bedroom, accepting his earlier invitation but on my own terms. Lying on the shelf beside the unfinished bust was a stack of apparently human hair, straight and black and long enough, I was sure, to sit atop the sculpture's head and drop down to its implied shoulders.

The hair beside the sculpture and the thinness of the face were enough to tell me the bust would be of either Sherilee Malcolm or Alice House, but which? Who was it Simon Parker was currently obsessed with? Was this face fully formed a few days ago, would I have seen it that way had I come in here when Parker had asked me to? And if I had seen it, would I have known who it was supposed to be? Could Parker tell the two women apart? Could I?

I drove downtown, timed my arrival at the Bank of America building for a quarter to five, waited for Alice's emergence. I sat across the street, double-parked, and watched the doors. At five to five the exodus began, and my eyes leapt from face to face as the crowd filled the sidewalk in twos threes and fours, the young groups smiling, the old men snarling. I looked past their farewell waves, watched each new escapee spit out by the revolving doors.

My attention rapt in that direction, I didn't notice until his horn blew that the man in the car beside mine wanted to leave his parking place. I pulled up to let him out, looked across the street for Alice, pulled up a little more. The car zipped out from behind me, nearly scraped my rear fender on its hurried way past. Now the car I'd pulled up next to wanted out. I checked my rear view mirror and was about to back into the newly vacated space when some lunatic tore around the corner and skidded suddenly to his right, claimed the space with the front of his car while the back half sat fishtailed into traffic. The car beside me, still wanting out, honked. Swearing under my breath, I eased forward. Into the woman who'd stepped in front of my car.

I put it in park and got out, stepped toward the woman who sat on her butt on the asphalt, purse still clinging to her shoulder.

I recognized the black hair and the angular pale face. I froze. I'd meant to bump into Alice House, but not like this.

"Are you alright?" I asked, forcing the bland necessary words out of my mouth.

"God, I hate Mondays," Alice answered, with the lightest of accents. She had left Texas long ago. "Help me up, will ya?"

She offered both hands together and I took them in mine. With a tug I brought her to her feet. She brushed dirt from the sides and back of her dress.

"Where were you hit?" I asked.

"A scratch," she drawled, "right here," and slapped herself on the right hip. "Ow. Should'na done that, I suppose."

"Do you want to see a doctor?"

"Only if he's buying me a drink. You a doctor?"

There were murmurs around us, a circle of vultures, gawking with obvious disappointment. I wondered where they'd come from and wished they'd go back.

"Let's get out of here," Alice said. "You normally drive better than that, don'tcha?"

"Yeah."

"Then drive me to drink. I know a place a few blocks from here."

We got in the car and I turned when she said to turn, parked where she said to park, not hitting anyone along the way. Of course, there was no one else I was following.

Running into Alice this way bothered me. How she'd managed to walk in front of my car from across the street without me seeing her leave the building, that bothered me too. And her wanting a drink with the man who'd hit her with his car didn't make sense, it felt like a set-up. But I was too suspicious to ever be set up. And here we'd met, that was the important thing, and we'd introduced ourselves to each other in the car, and now we were sitting in a crowded little bar South of Market, rock music playing loud enough to be heard but not so loud you had to shout over it. Alice had a martini, I had a beer. The bartender knew her by name, and she knew him the same, and she waved to some of the others there.

There weren't many people as old as me, and those that were looked a bit more ragged, less recently shaved and more recently out of work. My gray suit jacket stood out in the room full of leather, but enough of the women were pretty and I was with one of them, so I didn't mind not fitting in.

"Your kind of people?" I asked Alice.

She shrugged. "They like a good time, I like a good time. You?"

"What else is there to like?"

"All day long I talk to people who only like money. All night long I have to get away."

I nodded.

Alice's smile was small. "You think my hip's worth a second drink?"

I looked away from her face and saw her empty glass. "I think it's worth a lot more."

I ordered us both refills and finished my beer.

"So. Wash. That's a funny name."

"Short for Washington. Patriotic parents." One good thing about my first name, I never had to explain how the family earned the surname.

I wanted to kiss her thin lips and take her away from the bar, knew that was something I shouldn't do, not until I was sure Parker was stable and out of the way. But I might not be able to resist her that long.

Alice excused herself a minute to go to the bathroom. When she came back she wore a silver nose ring.

"Does that get in the way?"

"Of what?"

I grinned. "Inhaling. Whatever it is you inhale."

"Nothing but air. And sometimes I don't know about that."

Cigarettes burned everywhere. I took a deep breath, swallowed the taste of young lust, frustration, blues, nicotine and alcohol and dreams, hopelessness fucking hope. There was a chance for everything here, always a possibility. Alice House was no one I knew, and I was someone who'd hit her with a car, and that was all it took to bring people together. Bad luck was something you played with until it changed.

It was a euphoric moment, but it was only a moment.

"Look," I said, "you wanna get out of here?"

"And do what?" Alice grinned mischievously.

"Anything you want. Maybe go to a club and check out a band."

"Well, it's a little early for that," Alice said. "Let's have a couple more drinks first." She winked. "Then we can do anything I want."

Drinking with a pretty woman, her face pale and taut, her hair thin and black, her eyes dark, our drinks cold, the music getting better with each beer, I was doing nothing I hadn't done before, but this crowd was younger and dirtier than the people I usually allowed into my life. My only regret was I hadn't left my jacket in the car. I took it off, draped it over the bar stool, and sat.

She drank, I drank, everyone in the room drank. We talked to each other, with asides to the people around us, until the conversation, never intimate, grew vast. The more drinks flowed the louder we talked, the more people heard us and answered. Drunk, the night far from over, we drank and yelled and laughed, slapped the bar and our new friends' shoulders, until almost closing time and eight of us stood on the sidewalk deciding where to get more drinks and where to drink them.

Unsure who my new friends were and not really caring, I led Alice and two strangers into my car and we slowly followed the other foursome up the road, stopped quickly to buy some beers then rolled on down toward the house they swore was nearby.

It seemed to me, finding a parking place along the curb, that I'd somehow been sidetracked, but on the other hand, this scenic route might be the most direct path to Alice, a night that would show me as I was and show her as she was, with our guards down, so she could see what I was like, could see I was someone she could talk to.

We were crammed into a kitchen, drinking everything we'd bought, drinking fast talking fast and yes loud yes because we had points to make and each word had to overpower the words it overlapped. We were shouting strangers, in agreement but not quite, and the slightest difference of opinion had to be made clear.

Someone not here shouted through the open window: "Shut up in there!"

"Come on," one of our hosts gestured, leading us into the

adjoining living room, where three fast movers flopped onto a short couch, leaving the rest of us the floor. I yanked Alice down beside me and we sat together. There was only one other woman in the small room and she was with someone too. The rest of the guys had each other.

Excited conversation continued but I withdrew from it, looked at Alice, felt somehow a decision had been made, our initial attraction to each other had taken a step further, the curiosity with which Alice came to me now more definite than it had been when all she'd wanted from me was a drink.

"You know," I said softly to Alice when I saw her returning my stare, "I was supposed to meet you."

"You were?" She looked amused. "You mean this was meant to be?"

"No," I shook my head, "not like that." I drank some beer. "Someone I know said I should meet you."

"Who?"

"Simon Parker."

Alice didn't look surprised. "I didn't expect Simon to go fixing me up. Is that what he was doing? Or are we supposed to talk?"

"We're supposed to talk."

"Did he tell you where I work? Were you following me?"

"I was trying to find you when we met. I didn't see you coming, I swear."

"And I thought you ran me down to pick me up."

"I thought I'd try another method first."

Alice clicked her tongue. "You almost thought too much."

"So maybe we were supposed to meet. I'll accept providence."

"You don't have much choice. Well, now you got me, I bet you don't know what to do with me."

She was more than half right and I was more than half drunk, so I defended myself. "I know what I'd like to do."

Alice shook her head, slow and certain. "But you're not gonna do it."

"Not yet."

"Then what?"

Someone played a few notes from a plastic miniature saxophone he'd found, louder than anything I could have said, louder than the rest of the room. It looked like a toy but it blared like a car horn. One of the guys on the couch laughed, serenaded by this solo of random notes, drunken noise accompanied by show-off poses, and soon everyone was laughing, some unable to stop, the laughter building in volume and the sax playing louder so it wouldn't be drowned out.

There was a crash from somewhere in the back of the house. One of our hosts charged in that direction and we followed, stopped in the kitchen. The host stood still in the middle of the floor, swore at the single brick and shards of broken glass at his feet. The wall he faced still held the cracked, broken remains of a window.

We had trailed the group into the kitchen, and now we stood at the back of an arc that had formed around our host, whose name I didn't remember, with people to our right and left ahead of us whose names I didn't remember, the beer almost gone, three o'clock Tuesday morning in a stranger's house, and it looked like nothing more would happen here except possibly violence.

I already held Alice's hand. We backed quietly out of the room, said goodnight from the doorway, maybe being heard, maybe not.

"I guess you know where I live," Alice said, her drawl masked by slurred speech as she flopped into the front seat of my car.

I took the wheel. "Yeah, I know where you live. You know where it is from here?"

Alice shrugged and I turned the key, pulled away from the curb and slowly drove as straight as I could. I watched the street signs, looked for something I remembered, something to tell me which way to turn, something that would click and remind me not only where I was but of a backroad route to Alice's place. My mind was adrift, tired and seeking comfort. I looked at Alice beside me. All I had to do was take her home.

But it was past three in the morning and I was drunk out of my mind. I shouldn't be driving at all but I couldn't leave my car behind, I didn't even know where I was, and if I drove slow enough I should be able to stay out of trouble. Maneuvering to keep the car straight, looking up for something I knew, a street name looked familiar and I turned right, not sure why. I turned on the radio to keep alert, awake, flicked across the dial trying to find someone singing, not talking. Alice's eyes flickered, then hovered at half-mast.

"Shit," I said.

"Ain't nothing on the radio," she answered. She put her hand on mine on the dial. "You watch the road, I'll find something."

I let her hand rest there a moment, then returned my hand to its steadying two o'clock on the wheel.

I drove somehow, let the wheel control my hands, followed the roads invisible memories brought before me, knew this unfamiliar terrain was a course that at some time I must have traveled, that somewhere in my subconscious I knew a way out of here. I drove like my car was a toy being pulled on a string. And I heard nothing. Whatever Alice played was nothing.

I went along for the ride, until within a few blocks of Alice's apartment I saw where I was and reclaimed control, stopped to park when I saw an open space only a block from her building. As we walked, my arm around her thin waist, she fumbled in her purse for the keys, her hand in groggy triumph yanking them into view. Alice wedged the key into the hole, opened the door an inch and turned to face me. Her hand pushed lightly into my chest, warded me off.

"I have to sleep now," she said. "Call me."

Surprised at the rejection and too hammered to think of anything else, all I said was, "But I don't have your number."

"Get it from Simon. G'night, Wash."

Alice leaned forward awkwardly, kissed me on the cheek, and pulled her head back, wedged herself through the door and shut it in front of me. My hand sunk into the pocket containing the key to the building's front door, squeezed it, and let go. The hand came out of the pocket empty, and I stood on the doorstep, slowly clenched and unclenched my fists, frustrated, angry, with nothing to do. If all I'd wanted was to get drunk I could have stayed home and passed out by now. Which, if I wasn't going to get laid, was all I felt like doing. There was no way I was making that drive across town, not without at least some coffee. Too bad the hookers around here were too cheap to have rooms, not ones you could stay in. Shoot your wad and go, business is business. Shit. I had to get out of here.

I turned and walked back to the car. It was too dangerous to sleep in it there, without at least driving to a better neighborhood, but driving would be more dangerous. I crawled into the backseat and lay down.

CHAPTER 11
SARAH

I CREATED FOR MYSELF A PAST, REPLETE WITH A WORK HISTORY AND lovers. The problem was how thoroughly I could fall into these fictions. There were times I felt I'd never escape, times I believed what I'd made up. This was a positive when writing fiction, not so much when I wrote about myself. I didn't always know where the fiction ended and the truth began. That's okay if I can remember which of these people from my past were manufactured by the world, and which by my mind.

Not a great difference: the world was a thing I held in my head or for me it would not exist. I'd written as though autobiographically before, it wasn't much of a stretch to believe I had lived what I had written. If I hadn't, how would I have written it? A part of me had to have lived that life, life with a man I hadn't actually met who was an amalgam of numerous men I'd known. I assure myself this is not a sign of madness but the opposite. Sanity is a thing I clutch at, a bottle or a man or a woman. So many options when clutching.

Perhaps it's desperation, but Sarah Persia is a desperate woman, a woman who needs out of whatever she is in. Whatever I am in. I don't know how life is supposed to be lived, I was born without a handbook and, without a guide, I am left to survive the best ways I see fit.

I want to be a writer but I do not know myself as one, my lovers have been professors and others whose attempts to put words on a page have failed to achieve publication, except maybe in a local journal.

I graduated high school, but didn't qualify for the scholarships necessary to make college affordable; I read a lot as a teen, but not the things I was supposed to. I was too impressed with the world to think much of unworldly academia.

So I took my diploma and did what after high school, did what for the nearly two decades since? Waited tables for a while, too long really, but unreported tips can cover a lot of expenses, far more than I had, which is good because it meant my skirts didn't have to be too short and my smiles didn't have to be too phony, no matter how repugnant the dialogue I was confronted with.

I suppose I learned something in all those years of dealing with patrons; the trick is whether I can put it on a page. What have I learned about humanity, or at least about myself? Why do I remain single, what is it about my hedonism that requires my happiness to always conclude in isolation? Too many years of talking to men and them not talking back, of watching them walk away and realizing how little would be gone. Where were the epic heroes of film and Bob Dylan songs, strong loners who deep down needed one good woman. It turns out they were strong and silent because they had nothing to say, their muscles had gone to their heads. Oh, some seemed to work for a while, but in the end there was always a lack of emotional depth (also in the beginning but in the beginning there was hope). Now I'm looking for someone to talk to and they're looking to be left alone and, in the meantime, their sexual prowess is fading while mine gets confused. I don't think I'm all that damn mature—except compared to men—but I'm at an age where I'm supposed to be. I'm beginning to understand why some old women surround themselves with cats. Something to stroke, someone who's there but doesn't interrupt, and when they have nothing to say they don't talk. Of course, there's no sex, but that's why they sell vibrators. Maybe old age is meant to be lived out in fantasy—it's not meant to be lived out at 35.

I suppose I could take a more active interest in women, but physically I've already got what women have, and I need what I do not have. Maybe I should take a more active interest in the rest of my life and love will come to me, when I am achieving, when I am worth loving. I am not that now.

People talk too much and they forget why they are talking, what it is they want to say and want to hear. To be part of you, when I find the right you, the right second person informal. I've gone through one of those; not all men are assholes, but sometimes things don't work out.

His skin against mine was an amazing thing, even his mouth to my ears. When he would talk about dreams, about a better world, or even this world's despair, he cared about life and he loved me. He drank too much but so did I, our plans slowed by the clutter in both our minds. As it was mutual, the drinking did not present a problem, at least not the problem presented when only one lover can't stop drinking.

His name was Kent, a solid Midwestern name with no significance, it said nothing about him and he didn't say much either. Strong and silent, short and stocky with the beginnings of a beer gut, but a little bit of something soft was okay beneath his sturdy, muscular chest. His hair was dark and so was he, in complexion and attitude, well-tanned and burly from years of working construction, and angry from the same, angry with the small-minded people he often worked with and sometimes joked and drank with, angry at the sad world he saw pass by from his precarious position on a high girder, angry at the rich he worked for who had so much yet did not prevent squalor, angry because the hard manual labor that should have fulfilled him did not ease his anger with each blow of the hammer, did not cause it to dissipate under the sun's glare. It came home with him and went out with him. Kent was glad to come home to someone who agreed that the world's sad and poor were not wretched of their own accord, but he had difficulty explaining why it hurt him as it did, even if he conceded that it was his own pain he felt.

"I feel sorry for these people, and there's nothing I can do."

"You're not in the position," I agreed. "Maybe someday."

But for that someday to come Kent needed to do something, and he couldn't even see what there was to do.

"You'll never change anything working on someone else's crew."

"You think I don't know that?"

But Kent didn't have a dream that he knew how to realize, he eventually got his contractor's license but lacked the acumen to do much of anything with it; he wound up being a contractor on someone else's crew. I wasn't realizing my dreams either, so it was easy for our conversations of constructive criticism to turn accusatorial; toward the end it became all too common.

"You get damn righteous," he said, putting down his beer a second, "for someone who doesn't do anything either."

"But at least I know what I want to do."

"Then why don't you do it?!"

Acrimonious as this blather could get, it wasn't what drove us apart. It may even have kept us together awhile, our mutual lack of accomplishments, something to moan about over drinks. We were losers together, each of us needing someone uplifting, neither of us capable on our own. His bitching about his life and my bitching about mine turned neither of our lives around, and maybe if he'd done something typical like sleep with someone else and let me catch him at it that whole phase of self-destruction would have ended years earlier, but he was too nice to show that kind of mercy, and here I'm laying the blame on Kent because I lacked the perception and intelligence to catch myself before I'd fallen too far.

Too far. Too far to want to get up and go to work, to make my share of our money. I knew I owed it to Kent to bring in, but I also owed myself the opportunity to grow and our inability to save any money was stifling that—I needed a new line of work, I needed a new way of living.

Drunk every night, bitching every night, a little bit of fat showing but mostly on the inside, our brains were slow and our souls hard to reach. It wasn't so much what happened to us as what didn't, as we waited for things to happen.

"You know, other people actually do things," I said, sitting with a bourbon at the table in our perennially dark kitchen—we rarely turned on the light, there wasn't much to see except ourselves, and after a while we didn't want that. We knew what we looked like, bleary-eyed and hopeless.

"You," Kent answered, "used to be fun to get drunk with."

"Now we get- I know."

We looked at each other in the dark across that narrow table and for a moment we were almost sober, we saw all too clearly how much we'd fucked ourselves up, how we were barely better off than the winos Kent felt sorry for. We had a roof over our heads so physically we were protected, but spiritually we had nothing. No hope, nothing but a rented apartment and booze that kept running out. Fuck, we were killing each other and we knew it.

We were born with a world of potential. Not everyone gets that chance, and we were blowing ours.

"We're in this hole together, Kent. Don't you want out?"

"Of course." His palms covered his eyes and cheeks, forehead leaned on bent fingers, their tips in his hair: "Who wouldn't want out?"

I couldn't see his face but didn't need to, thought I might never need to again.

I asked anyway. "Do you want out with me?"

He raised his head so his eyes peered out. "How?" His hands dropped from his face and held each other around his beer. "It's not like we haven't tried. And don't tell me this is self-pity, I don't have any ideas right now—"

"You never have any ideas."

"Shut up!" he barked, but now his voice dropped. "It's too late, I'm tired."

"You're always tired. Maybe it is too late."

"That's not what I meant." He shook his head sadly. "But you're right. This wears me out, I see it does you too. You don't need this, Sarah. You don't need me like this. I don't like me this way, why should you? I need to start over, whatever that means. I need—"

He stopped, took a drink. I tried to look at him, his face different now. I'd never seen him cry but now sensed he might. He drank a little longer and when he looked at me he looked drained. Somewhere behind that ruddy lost face was a man I used to know.

"I'm thinking of leaving California," he said.

"Where?"

"New Mexico. It's beautiful."

I nodded. We both knew you can't live on beautiful. We lived in California; a lack of beautiful was the least of our problems. "When?"

He shook his head and there were still no tears but I almost saw them anyway.

"I'm not asking you to come with me."

I looked down. "I know."

The floor was dark but so was Kent's face and I knew which one I would have to get used to. "Good luck," I said.

"Will you be okay?"

I looked up at his face once more, tried to find the handsome courage I once imagined there.

"You have to believe I will," I answered.

Neither of us was walking out the door right then, neither of us was leaving the room, we were stuck there together knowing it was over, knowing we'd sleep beside each other tonight. We weren't even mad, but sentence had been pronounced; as a couple we were dead, and I could not imagine anything more alone than being in this room with Kent. But neither of us left, all we did was drink, and the room held us tight like a slow gas leak. All I could do was hope to soon sleep, and hope when I woke that he would be gone.

CHAPTER 12
WASH

"So," I said, popping open my soda can, "I take it you know about Simon and Sherilee Malcolm."

Alice looked up from her salad. "I know about the shooting, if that's all you mean."

"About all," I said, taking a large, slow bite from my sandwich. We were in a café/sandwich shop down the street from where she worked.

"About?" Alice flung back hair that hadn't been in her face. "I only get a half-hour lunch, Wash. You best ask your questions."

"Okay," I smiled. "Did you know Simon initially made a positive identification, but was no longer sure by the time of the trial?"

"Hell, Wash, I was at the trial."

I straightened, spoke without finishing my bite. "Looking like that?"

Alice laughed. "Be a bit tacky, wouldn't it?" She straightened too. "My hair was blonde."

"But now…"

"It's sort of a tribute."

"You look like her on purpose."

"Well, since I look like her anyway…"

I swallowed but my throat was dry. I took a drink and tried again. "But when you went out with Simon—weren't you concerned what he might want from you?"

Alice took a drink of her own, shook her head slightly. "I was more concerned, like you say, with what I wanted from him. He had a hard time having a good time, that's all."

"But weren't you worried he might be thinking of her while making love to you?"

"We never got serious enough for worries."

"Did you consider he might be crazy?"

Chewing a small bite of salad, Alice smiled shutmouthed and shook her head. "I thought he was sad. Nothing crazy about that."

"But he was interested in you because you resembled someone he saw commit a murder."

"That's not why he liked me."

"He wasn't sure if Sherilee Malcolm killed Otto Workman, but he knew someone who looked like her did. Hell, maybe it was you. Did he ever treat you like a suspect?"

"Like you're treating me now?" Alice took a bite and shook her head again.

"Sorry," I said. "I need to know."

"Uh huh."

"I do. I don't trust Simon. What he might do."

"No telling what any man might do," Alice said. "What makes Simon special?"

"He may have witnessed another murder."

Alice cleared her throat. "Go on."

"Simon isn't sure what he saw, if he saw. One night last week he was drinking, he passed out, he might've dreamed the whole thing."

"What whole thing?"

"He thinks he saw a stabbing in an alley."

I watched Alice's face for a reaction. She stopped eating, but gave no indication of panic or guilt.

"Where?"

"He doesn't remember. But the killer looked something like Sherilee Malcolm."

Alice's voice dropped. It was barely above a whisper. "Something like," she murmured.

"He described her, didn't say it was her."

"Then it could've been me. That's what you're saying."

"The way he described the killer, it could've been you."

The old volume returned to her voice, but the tone remained empty. "That's nuts. There might be types of folks who go around stabbing folks in alleys, but I'm not one of them."

"I never thought you were. It's what Simon believes. But he doubts it too, can't be sure he saw anything."

"You really think he's crazy."

"I think there's a good chance."

Alice stabbed a chunk of lettuce with her fork and chewed it slowly. "And what do you do if he is?"

"Depends. I think he should see a doctor. Most important, I think you should stay away from him."

The smile was slight, the twang in her voice exaggerated. "Are you going to protect me?"

"I'd like to see you whether you need protection or not. It may be less pleasant than a date under normal circumstances, but we don't have that choice. Are you busy tonight?"

"Hell, Wash, I'm tired now. I wanna go home and sleep."

"How about I give you a few hours after work to nap, pick you up with some Chinese take-out, we eat it at your place, and you kick me out at your discretion."

Alice nodded, with a faint grin of acquiescence. "Alright."

"Alright? Good. Although, really, I think my place would be safer for you."

"Safer from Simon, maybe."

I wondered how much I'd have to protect Alice, how much of a security threat Simon was to the agency, how much of a job threat he was to me, how crazy he was. So far I could control him, so far I could get the better of him using words, but the time might come soon...I wondered what I'd have to do.

I had never had to kill anyone, didn't know if I could. Or if I should. It should have been up to Simon whether he'd become a victim, but I might not have time to see how crazy he was going. If he leaned in that direction he'd have to be stopped before he started.

We sat on one of Alice's two-seat couches, eating Chinese food. We'd pulled out the corner table and set it in front of us.

Alice wiped something off her mouth.

"What night," she asked, slowly, "did Simon see whatever he saw this time?"

"He talked to the police Tuesday night. Why?"

Alice blinked rapidly. "Maybe he did see something. Maybe he isn't crazy. He was drunk, he coulda got the description wrong, but maybe he saw something."

I leaned back. "But he doesn't know where and he doesn't know when. If there was corroborating evidence he'd be easier to believe. But there isn't. No one found any bodies."

"But I—" Alice stopped blinking, wet-eyed. She held her beer with both hands, brought it to her lips but held it there, stared at me a moment, then forced her eyes shut. They stayed that way as she slowly lowered the bottle to a place on the edge of the table.

Her head dropped down. Her lashes lifted, allowed her a view of the speck of floor she mumbled to.

"Last Tuesday I went drinking after work, and the last thing I remember I was still in the bar. Then I woke up here, hungover. I slept bad, I had crazy dreams, but I couldn't remember what they were. I need to know, Wash. What if I did something that night and Simon saw it, and I don't remember and he does, so he gets called crazy. What if I killed someone?"

Alice shook, held back tears.

I took her lean fingers in my hands and looked down toward her eyes. At last they looked back, blinking. I waited until they stopped.

"A lot of people have drunken blackouts." I forced a smile. "A lot more than commit murder."

Alice shook her head. "I was drinking tequila. It's different then. I do things…"

"Like what?"

Again she shook her head. "I can get…crazy. Sometimes I throw things. Break things."

"It's a long way from killing someone."

"Depends if someone's there to stop me."

She was too worried, she was leaving something out. "Do you carry a knife?"

"No."

"Would you wander down an alley with someone you couldn't stand?"

"Might if I was drunk enough. To get high or something."

"You're not building much of a case against yourself."

"It's the coincidence, me and Simon blacking out the same night. If it was the same night. Do you know if it was Tuesday? It's one of those things makes you worry."

"It might have been Monday, he didn't say," I lied, "but maybe you shouldn't drink tequila. Or keep me around when you do. I'd like to see you when you might do anything."

"No you wouldn't. The stuff inside me's buried for a reason."

It looked like we weren't solving anything tonight. I didn't mind. I already believed what I wanted to know. Alice was no killer. She was something else. I smiled.

Alice frowned. "I'd like to take a walk if we're done eating. Before this food settles and bloats me."

"A short walk, I hope."

"Don't worry, I don't have any energy. If I laid down now I'd go right to sleep."

"Let's walk."

Alice stood, and crossed the room to retrieve her jacket from the closet. When she turned around, holding the jacket over her right shoulder, I was in front of her. I put one hand on her shoulder and the other on her cheek and we kissed. The brown leather jacket dropped to the floor.

I woke up sweating, my arms wrapped tightly around Alice, my fingernails digging into my palms. I released the bent aching fingers, stretched them outward, allowed them to once again reach for something.

But I already had all I could reasonably expect to get in one night: pleasure, comfort, someone I needed needing me. Not that it was her in particular I needed. I kissed the top of Alice's head, repositioned an arm that had fallen asleep, and closed my eyes again, knowing I could usually count on sleep as a place to find peace.

But sleep wasn't easy. That doubt inside of Alice, that fear, it wasn't the sort of thing caused by one drunken night. Maybe she was a little bit crazy. Not murderous of course, but neurotic.

Of course neurotic. She was with me. Not that she'd stay, no one ever stayed, the woman always left or I did, as anyone would leave. Walking away was what people like us did. That was why we were together now, because we needed to be and because we knew it wouldn't last, we didn't have to worry about that. So we'd had a beautiful night, and we could have some more. For now we had to hold on. Later we would have to let go.

Dreams were strange, kept half-waking me uneasy, unable to

remember what they were. Exhausted by all this half-sleep, I finally passed out as light from the rising sun crept into the room.

I woke alone, wondered where she'd gone, lay awake in the dim light waiting for her return. Closed my eyes, hoped to find a few more restful minutes. I lay there on my side, my hand stroking the sheet where Alice should've been. I turned onto my back, grabbed my pants from the floor, flopped my legs over the side of the bed and got half-dressed.

Shirtless I walked out of the bedroom, expected to see Alice in the living room or kitchen, but both rooms were empty. The bathroom door was closed. I knocked but there was no answer.

"You in there, Alice?"

Still no answer. I opened the door—no one. Figuring she must have gone down to get a paper or something, I took a leak then returned to the bedroom, unsure of the time, of whether I should maybe be prowling the kitchen for coffee.

I glanced at the clock, saw it was still damn early, dropped my pants back to the floor and resumed my uncertain position under the blankets, wanting to sleep but wanting to fuck even more, and for the moment unable to do either.

I lay awake on my side, on my back, on the other side, on my belly, wanting Alice.

And then her hand was on my arm, shaking me lightly from behind. I rolled over and kissed her, asked her where she'd been.

"Right here," she answered, sounding surprised.

"But I was up a little while ago and you weren't here. You weren't anywhere."

"You musta been dreaming. Unless there's a fire or earthquake I don't go anywhere undressed."

"God, it seemed so real. Goddamn dreams."

We kissed again, and it was true she wasn't dressed, at least not now. We made love again, desperately reasserted our passion of the night before, a reminder that we remained capable of tenderness, at least some animal version of it.

"I have to get back to the office today." We'd freed ourselves of each other and sat in the kitchen drinking coffee. "I'm past deadline."

Alice took a sip, nodded as though she understood. But did I understand? My deadline was past and I'd solved nothing, all I was sure of was Alice had committed no murder. I knew nothing of what had actually happened to Simon Parker that night. Was Parker a crazy man, dangerously crazy, a threat to agency security? Or worse, a threat to Alice?

"Where's your phone?" I asked as Alice poured refills.

"On the table between the couches."

I found it on the living room floor, where the table had been before we'd moved it to eat. It was late enough for Hutcheson to be in his office, and with a full cup of coffee, I could wait as long as he could leave me waiting.

"Sally," I said when the old man's secretary answered, "it's Wash. Can you put me through?"

"A minute," she said, and I could see pink painted nail pushing the button, putting me on hold. At least no music played.

I sipped the coffee slow, tried to put the words in order so they would come out strong enough to persuade the old man. I'd drunk half the cup when Hutcheson's hard voice came on the line.

"What is it, Shank?"

Deference wouldn't work, Hutcheson too blunt to acknowledge it.

"I need a little time to wrap up the Parker case. One more day and it'll be settled."

"You have until noon to get here. I suggest you settle matters now."

"Yes, sir. Thanks."

"Be here at noon." He hung up.

With the remains of my coffee, I returned to the kitchen. Alice stood at the stove, cooking eggs and smoking a cigarette. She turned her head over her shoulder, looked at me with one dark eye. "Well?"

"Do you know what time Simon leaves in the morning?"

"I'm sure he gets there late as he can. Why?"

"I gotta go." I crossed the room and kissed her cheek.

"Now? I can't eat all these eggs."

"I'll buy you a chicken later."

"Thanks, Wash. Christ. You always leave this fast?"

"I have to find Simon."

Alice swiveled around and gave me a real kiss. "Come back soon, okay?"

"I wouldn't leave if I didn't have to."

I threw the rest of my clothes on fast and got out of there before I wound up staying, pulled my coat on as I walked down the hall. I pounded on Parker's door, unsure of what I was going to say but eager to get things over with. I waited a minute, pounded again. I heard a growl inside, then trudging footsteps.

"What?!" Parker barked from behind the door.

"Simon, it's me, Wash. I gotta talk to you."

"Come back tonight."

"It has to be now."

"Why?"

"Let me in. I'm not telling you from the hall."

I heard the bolt pull back, the doorknob unlock. The door opened wide and I stepped in warily.

Parker stood there naked and hairy, a large beast awakened in its lair. He slammed the door shut. "This better be fucking good."

He turned his back on me and strode into the bedroom, returned wearing a paint-stained pair of Levi's.

"I'm trying to find out if you're crazy, Simon. If you're crazy or you blacked out. One drunk night. Because I'm sure Alice House didn't kill anybody. I've talked to her."

"I bet you have," he said, taking the only chair, leaving me to stand. "Alice House. That's great. You fucked her, didn't you?

Then you decided anyone who fucked you was too nice to be a killer. Maybe you have too low a self-image. You're not the only guy Alice ever fucked, you know."

"You're talking nonsense, Simon."

"And you're turning red, Wash. What did you expect me to do when you came in here? Confess I'm crazy, or be crazy? Tell you not to worry about it, I was drunk that one night but that's all it was, everything's fine now? Whatever gets your girlfriend off the hook, is that it?"

I shook my head. "If you acting crazy was going to make me happy, I'd be ecstatic. Listen to yourself, Simon. We need to have a rational conversation. Of course it's about Alice, but it's more about you. You and what you see in her, and whether the sudden reemergence of Sherilee Malcolm in your mind is dangerous."

"You do think I'm crazy, don't you Wash? But I'm not the one who ran in front of your car to meet you.—Ah, you look surprised. You didn't still think that was an accident, did you? I thought by now Alice would tell you these things."

"She ran? But how? She knew who I was?"

"She left that out, too? She was with me the day I saw you in the street. The day I followed you. I'm sure she was curious when she saw your car."

"But why didn't you tell me? I was investigating her for you."

Parker brushed invisible flecks off the thighs of his jeans. His eyes gleamed. "I thought it would be more interesting this way. You thinking she didn't know who you were, what you were. What you are. And if this is all news to you, I guess she's still working on you. You know, the more I think about her the easier it is to believe what I saw."

And the harder it is for me, I should have said. What he saw. What he knew about Alice, and what did I know about her? She was someone who had misled me from the start. As I had misled her. And she knew exactly what I was doing. Yet even when I told her Parker had wanted me to meet her, even when I told her he thought she had committed murder, she did not answer in kind, she did not tell me she had known my line of work from the beginning. Didn't say she had arranged to meet me. Why had she? I didn't doubt Parker's word on this; it was clearly a truth he took great pleasure in telling. I stood silent before him, unable to defend Alice or my own belief in her. Shaken.

Parker was silent too, I don't know how long.

"Then," I said, ashamed to ask but asking, "do you really believe you saw her kill someone?"

"I don't know," he answered, the last word spoken with an indignant smile. "You're supposed to find that out for me."

But how could I find out she was definitely innocent? If she was guilty there might be evidence, but if she'd done nothing, how could that be proved? If there had been a murder and the body disappeared, or if there'd been no killing at all, the same lack of evidence remained. If Alice didn't know, and it was up to me to convince her, to believe in her...

When Alice and I had talked about it, I'd had no doubts.

Now I had to talk to Alice about the things Parker had told me. I had to ask her about it, but I knew it would be true. That it was true. That she'd met me knowing who I was, that she'd thrown herself not only at me but at my car, that she may have fucked me to allay my suspicions of her. Only I hadn't been suspicious then.

The subject had to be changed. It was early in the morning and my mind wasn't working, it was still under the influence of dreams. I had little time, I had to think quickly. I remembered Alice disappearing, if only in a dream, then reappearing, if only for me. I closed my eyes a moment, opened them, wanted to see Alice where Simon was but instead saw only flickering colors. Then all was clear and again I saw Simon. I looked at my wrist, but I wore no watch. And I saw something else.

I raised my eyes. "Tell me something, Simon."

"Yeah, what?"

"About your experiment with the lights. What is it, really? What is it supposed to do?"

Parker stretched his broad arms and sat back as much as he could in his lone little chair. He spoke slowly.

"The intent is to produce hallucinogenic effects. By programming the movement of the blocks to create a combination of motion and light, I'm attempting to free the subconscious mind." He smiled. "It may even work as a memory device."

"So, when you looked into the lights and saw Sherilee Malcolm—"

"It was no accident. It was the reason behind the device's creation."

"You needed to see her face again."

"To bring it out of the shadows. Now," Parker sighed, "it can't haunt me anymore."

"And," I said, "there was something else you were trying to remember. Did that come to you too?"

Parker looked relaxed. The anger dropped from his eyes, and he smiled like it was a natural thing for him to do. "To quote Lynyrd Skynyrd," he answered, "'you got that right.'"

The smile widened, the words stopped. Again he had the upper hand, and I was forced to make him play it.

"What else did you see, Simon? Did you really see a second murder?"

"It must have been a dream. Alice told me she didn't do it."

"Alice told you?"

Parker nodded, smiling.

I looked at his calm face. "And if she lied and killed someone?"

The smile was all teeth. "She wouldn't lie to me."

I took a deep breath. Simon Parker was my client. His and the agency's security were my assignment, and now I was certain of both. This had all been revenge, a little trick Parker had played on my mind. To make me doubt myself. And Alice. And it had worked, temporarily. But at the same time, I had completed my assignment. I was good at my job, and if that meant nothing would come of meeting someone like Alice, so be it. It was only through the job that we had met, and while some of what we shared was truth, deceit always lay between us. I had broken into her apartment, read her personal papers, and followed her, and we had each pretended not to know the other when we met. And we had gotten as far as we had dishonestly, as probably most people do, the difference being that each of us had discovered the other's lies. At least some of them. They were nothing accidental, and I could not promise honesty in the future. It all depended on the job. I didn't know what Alice could promise, what she might promise.

I took another deep breath. "You're no threat to agency security, are you, Simon?"

"No, not at all," Parker answered with a wide grin. "I'm not a dangerous person."

He had won, there was nothing more he needed to do to me.

"I don't think you have to worry about your sanity either," I said, softly.

"I worry only about my art. The creation of Sherilee reassured me about my mind."

I faced the floor, raised my head slowly to speak to him once more. "Then I don't think you need me on your case any longer."

"But what about Alice?"

I hesitated. I knew there was something wrong with me not trusting her. If it was all in my mind, that was no consolation. It was no longer Parker's sanity I doubted, but Alice's word.

"I'll never prove her guilty or innocent," I answered. "All I have on that is my own belief."

I turned and walked to the door, opened it.

"And what do you believe?" Simon asked from his seat behind my back.

I stepped into the hall and shut the door.

CHAPTER 13
SARAH/SHERILEE

RON PAINTS, BUT WHAT DOES HE PAINT? WHAT HE SEES, AS WHAT HE senses. He knows he is not yet succeeding on his own terms, and that is important. I have met other artists recently, and they all talk about their art in terms of themselves. And you have to be too damn good if you're going to make every painting a self-portrait.

But to make it to Saturday morning and Ron it seemed I first had to talk to all these paint-by-numbers artists, limited successes in all walks of life. And this by my definition of success, nothing to do with money, something to do with facing things. Something I was learning to do.

"But it doesn't matter if I capture what I set out to," said one, "so long as I capture something."

"You sound like a fucking zookeeper." I didn't stick around.

Because it's hard to know what you want, but to not know and claim it doesn't matter, then take credit for whatever happens to you, is not the combination of intelligence and humility I wish to keep in my company.

The problem with Ron may be that he only glimpses the terror he sees as essential to his art, but at least he knows he only glimpses it, knows there is something else there. Some of these others, with their clear views of horror and beauty and how the two mesmerizingly intermingle...well, I can't help doubting them and asking them to sketch something on a napkin to give me an idea of their visions.

"I don't do that," he said, one hand brushing stringy black hair from his eyes. "I'm an artist, I have to be inspired."

"Draw me a dog," I said. "Or a drooling leper. Or James Dean, or Madonna or *The Madonna*. Something vulgar, something sacred. Whatever turns you on."

"Okay," he grinned, "got a pen?"

My smile, I assumed, was wistful. From my purse I withdrew a handful of pens and handed him one, returned the remainder to their pouch.

"You must write a lot."

"My diary. I'm compulsive."

He unfolded his napkin and began to draw, a naked woman on a motorcycle. It was done quickly and not too badly; that is, I could tell the chick from the hog.

"Impressive," I said, "you know her?"

"Naw," he grinned proudly, "but I have a bike. You wanna check it out?"

"I don't ride with men I don't know."

"I'll buy ya a drink."

"Are all your pictures this inspired?"

He shook his head, flapped his hands. "If I spend some time with a beautiful woman, I wind up drawing a beautiful woman."

"Uh huh." I nodded. "I'll get my own drink."

Sometimes people get pissed off when the conversation goes too long, and I realize I'm talking to too many men. They always expect promises to be made, or at least wish they could expect them. But making promises is exactly what I don't want to do. I want to find the truth. I can't claim that I have it, or expect it from anyone else, or give up on it too soon.

But I don't want the truth of a creep, the truth as seen by someone jaundiced or moronic, or any other truth that isn't similar to mine. I am my mystery, and I do not expect to be solved without the help of someone insightful and intelligent. And I know even then I won't get to the mystery's depths, that the process will be an unfolding, but it is a process that must begin, and alone I seem incapable even of such beginnings.

Somewhere I picked up a coffee to go, somewhere narrow and not crowded, a coffee dive. The taste was less than spectacular, but the caffeine would take away my headache and there was no scene.

It was a lack I sought, a stepping out onto the sidewalk and seeing no one who wanted to be anything. It was ugly, and these were losers, and this was death, and my view was lovely.

People you didn't talk to unless you wanted to get fucked up, one way or another. They filled the street, worthy of pity unless they got in your way, then worthy of hate. They were already in oblivion and saw no reason not to inflict it on anyone else; theirs was a world beneath reason.

I found a cigarette in the pack in my purse and lit the goddamn thing, knowing these pitiable creatures had become that, creatures; although they remained human, they might not act that way, not at least the way of those constrained by society. They might strike me for my cigarette, might be foolish enough to attempt to snatch my purse. But by many standards, I too was mad, in my case an especially apt term because of the anger in my insanity, and I would likely cripple anyone who tried to rob me.

I stood feral on that street corner, watched the others around me, watched the cars follow the streetlights, watched the ash drop from my cigarette to the sidewalk, watched over my hot paper cup as I raised its lip to mine.

A child draws, hand atop pen, delighted with her doodling, the shapes she can make.

Now we no longer wonder at the stray shape or its making, but must make or say something in particular, in the belief that we can so we must, or the greater belief that we cannot but we must anyway.

Not having time to read, or to write, having time only to live. And knowing that in recent years I have lived only as research: one step removed.

> "The thinker, and the artist likewise, who has secreted his better self in his works, feels an almost malicious joy when he sees how his body and his spirit are being slowly broken down and destroyed by time; it is as though he observed from a corner a thief working away at his money-chest, while knowing that the chest is empty and all the treasures saved."
>
> NIETZSCHE (*HUMAN, ALL TOO HUMAN*)

For years I'd carried the card containing those lines. Now I found it in my purse, and flipped it to the sidewalk.

Of course, I could still quote the words by heart.

I piled into the back of a large already full car, it was night and I again needed a crowd. I didn't know who these people were, only that they were fun to drink with, and a group was probably less dangerous than one person.

The dangers I was avoiding were the physical ones. A group

of course is more likely to contain an asshole, but I'd have been very much surprised to meet anyone who could psychologically damage me more than I already was.

Damaged. 'Tis to laugh, my dear. The barrooms run rampant with the damaged, specializing in inflicting pain on themselves and leaving little impression on anyone else.

Crammed between the door and a dark brunette I hadn't been talking to, I felt suddenly empty as the car veered away from the curb. I didn't want to talk to anyone, only to be with someone. I ached, and shivered as much as the tight quarters allowed.

"You cold?" asked the brunette. Her hair was almost black, her eyes light brown.

"Alright," I murmured. I forced a grin, realized my teeth were clenched. "Been colder."

She grinned back, and a brief glint of white teeth accentuated her face's light tan.

I wondered why I'd barely noticed her before. "I'm Sarah," I said, the smile relaxing. "Sarah Persia, the renowned unpublished novelist."

"Jean," she answered. "I heard your name before."

"I," I stammered, "I'm not exactly famous."

Jean's head shook quickly. "I meant tonight. What do you write?"

I shrugged, back to almost normal. "Bad poetry, I guess. Like everyone else. A diary. I don't know. I'm not sure writing's what I should do."

"It's up to you," Jean said, and I felt her arm pressed against mine. "But you said you had an unpublished novel."

Oops. "Yeah, well, it's not exactly finished. And don't even ask me what it's about. I guess if I could describe it I wouldn't be writing it."

"You should show it to people. It doesn't matter if they don't like it, maybe they'll feel it."

I guessed Jean's age at thirty. "What is it *you* do?" I asked.

"Like everyone else around here," she answered—inside the car was a din but we were close enough we didn't have to yell— "not what I want. But I put out a zine. Give me something small, I'll try to fit you in."

Exactly what I didn't want, but it didn't have to matter. What I wanted was more immediate.

"Come to my place sometime," I said, watching the unflickering pale brown eyes. "I've got tons in a folder."

"I don't have room for tons. Pick out the best ounce and bring it to me."

I nodded in agreement. "Alright."

I sat there in my new corner of the literary underground and listened to the words of strangers.

"You're kicking a dead horse. Most movies suck, and men make them. I don't care if it's a coincidence. *It's our turn.*"

"It was a man's book to begin with."

"Not really. It was only written by a man."

I heard myself everywhere.

"What's it like putting out a zine?"

"Time-consuming, occasionally productive. It's like having a retarded kid. I love it, and I know how little it can do."

I laughed. "It's strange, thinking you know what you're creating."

"It isn't there," Jean said. "What you think, what you know."

We're stuck with words. We don't even know what they mean. The ones we're sure of, think we grasp; doesn't matter: they're different to someone else, communication collapses.

"What's it called?" I asked.

"*Pen,*" she paused for emphasis, "*Noir.*"

I smiled. "I like it. But I haven't seen it."

Jean nodded. "Distribution's a bitch."

"So am I. Maybe I can help."

The car stopped outside a liquor store and drunkenly we clambered out, a gang of adults too old for this sort of thing and very much enjoying it.

A slow groove instilled itself in us as we entered the store. Businesslike we made our selections, bought our booze and got out.

I opened my bottle outside the store, took a slug and passed it to Jean.

"Cap it," she said.

I took another slug and did what I was told, dropped the small bag into my purse. I shrugged. My eyes felt light, I felt them flicker. I was enjoying myself, even while engendering small hostilities in someone I thought I liked.

I turned casually, felt a wound within, spun and lurched and vomited falling forward, stumbling sideways to keep the puke off my clothes, spewed the gross spittle from my lips, caught myself against the side of the car.

"You alright?" someone asked.

"Got any breath mints?" I answered.

"You need a cab?" another asked.

"Fine, fine." I cleared my throat, shook my head, and spit onto the street. "It wasn't the booze."

I shook my head again, reached into my purse for something to wipe my mouth. "I'm okay. Let's go."

You don't know how good it is, he said, to turn on the radio and hear something you like, something it seemed like you were the only one who liked. To start your day that way. It makes up for that woke-up, "feel like I got tiger balm in my eyes" feeling.

What is it you like that no one else likes?

And the answer isn't free jazz, or grunge, or folk or country or easy listening. There are sexual and other pleasures, first admit them to yourself, your sadistic and masochistic needs.

Don't deny the manic-depressive, schizophrenia can be your friend, can replace all your old friends.

I drank water, then traded my bourbon for some beer. Still convinced it wasn't the alcohol made me sick, but everything I'd done was an ingredient in my chemical imbalance, and some of it needed to be countered. Or I needed to throw up more, the poison may have been what was coming out. I stretched, and rubbed my tight neck. Some form of clarity, some kind of health, would or had come to me.

Not knowing what was going on was the usual, and acceptable, so long as I could continue to observe.

Music played. I asked what it was, was told Nirvana. This I doubted, but it was alright.

My hands grew cold. Immersed in pop culture, I needed a hot drink.

"Got any coffee?" I asked.

We were in a house shared by a woman and a man. I could not tell if they were lovers; they were at least close friends. One of them said yes, and the other rose to start some coffee, asked the room if anyone else wanted some.

The walls were painted black and red, wide, alternating vertical stripes. The living room was not large, but large enough, with two soft couches and comfort to be found even on the floor. When I stood to join my host in the kitchen, I knew that any clamor would not be a fight for my vacated cushion but the noise of conversations colliding.

"You didn't want decaf, did you?" So glib, so facile, so in-control. As though I were a situation.

"God no," I played along, momentarily repulsed by us both.

"Artificial stimulation it is." He turned slowly, three steps returning him to the counter, where he took a brief, brown drink from a clear, short glass before resuming his preparations.

"No one takes responsibility," I said.

As though there were autonomy. Again, it seemed to me the attempt at free will more important than if it existed.

Midmorning silence, for morning started at midnight, and a crack in the curtain let in hints of dawn. The sun would soon sit astride the horizon, we would see all too clearly. True darkness, hidden in shadows, stands out in bright light.

"You seem to dislike people," he smiled. "I mean, for someone who is one."

"There's someone worth liking," I answered. "At least, there was."

"Was?"

"One person dies, I assume he isn't the only one."

Light crept around the curtain like a horde of insects: slow, irritating, and everywhere. I blinked at it, but it didn't go away.

"Will the coffee be here before morning?" I asked.

"Too late for that."

I was stuck in a conversation and I'd go to bed alone, this was not what I wanted. To race airily out of the kitchen with my coffee cup and charm one of those potential lovers with my breezy devil-may-care attitude; oops, not me. But I wanted it to be, and this was what I was attempting, to be someone else. I waited for the coffee. If I was going to transform myself I would at least need fuel.

I needed to write and I knew I needed to write. Inside I was crumpled like a paper ball. All I was writing these days was a diary, and it wasn't enough. My mundane existence, however insane I made it, did not interest as much as would that of a fictional character. That's what I was trying to overcome now, and boring moments like this were the greatest challenge.

I didn't know my host's name. I thought he'd probably said it, and I didn't want to ask. Sometimes an entire night begins to feel like someone you've slept with once, and once too often. To talk now didn't seem so great, to barge into that other room a waste of time; I'd only lose whatever I'd thus far gained.

I stood, sagging, at the shoulders at the knees in the chest, on the verge of rolling forward, wanting to. No longer wanting to be me, to be judged as me or any other human, not enough to swim through criticism, even that only implied because I had flaws. Wanting only not to be.

Could not be in this place any longer, but nowhere would be better. Therapy! I screamed, but only in my head, and with a gasp of relief fell to the floor.

———

I don't know who I am, as though someone else has lived my life before me, leaving me with only the unwanted remnants: emptiness, no friends, a lack of self-knowledge. All I have is amnesia, and the certainty that I am a failure as a writer, my words only scribbles, barely decipherable.

Yet my inability to discover myself is mirrored, almost mockingly, by a writer who seems to unveil me with every word: Sherilee Malcolm, the woman they say killed Otto Workman, although I can't believe that; Sherilee Malcolm, whose words haunt my memory although I don't remember reading them. She seems to know me, she even looks like me if I changed the color of my hair. That too is a memory, and I remember so little, why this insistence that I resemble a stranger?

She reveals to me who I am, takes me where I have gone, shows me what I have seen. I do not remember until I am shown, it is as though without her to point the way I am an insentient being, a creature incapable of using what I have. I am the cipher, adrift without qualities and unable to accrue them, but I do have qualities, if only hers. A life secondhand. To always follow, to never be; capable but unable to locate those capabilities, like a baby unable to grab because I am unaware of my hands. I am nothing but a parasite dependent on this other woman. Somehow she lives and communicates to me, and in her writing fools me into momentarily believing that I live too. But I cannot.

How does she do this, how does she know so much about me? Has she somehow robbed me of my memory, that she may use it for her books? Her works of fiction? This is my life she has taken, and I want it back. Perhaps if I could find her, for it is me she writes about; she knows the rest of my life, she must give it to me.

I know there is something wrong with this, something that even through this haze must connect, something that I fathom but is out of reach, and I have had too much to drink and I lie here on this couch and my head is capable of settling and returning to me information that I know is there, is almost here.

I close my eyes and turn onto my side, away from the light. But when I open my eyes to see where that light is coming from, through what hidden window, there is no light, all is dark. I fear that death approaches, that is what sleep holds for me.

But it cannot be the end of Sarah Persia, for I do not know who I am, and what kind of insanity is this that does not grant the mercy of self-knowledge before death? Where is a life to flash before my eyes? I remember nothing but the last few days, and I know even in this short span much of what I have said is lies, not because I was protecting myself from the pain of the truth but because I do not know the truth. If I can tell only what I know I will remain mute; I must talk of what I do not know, I must imagine what my life could be.

It is frightening to know that I may meet someone who knows me, who will recognize me yet I may not know them, there are only the people I have met in the last week or so. And what if that is as long as my memory is good for, and in another week I must start again?

I cannot live that way, I must assume that it is only through some great accident that I have lost who I once was, and that the woman I build now will be as permanent as any other. But what do I do? I lie here on this couch fearing death, feeling queasy, not knowing how much of this feeling is physical, knowing that the sun had begun to rise before I passed out and that when I leave here it will not be into darkness that I walk.

I suppose I require help, but I do not want sympathy, I want to do this myself, even those things I seem incapable of doing. Especially those. For this amnesia need not be taken as tragedy but as opportunity, a fresh start that many my age no doubt wish they could make. Whatever my age may be. Mid-thirties, I would guess, but unhindered by birth records or identification papers I can claim any age that is convenient.

But do I have no identification? I have a purse, and a wallet within. I open it and tremble. Do I want to know who I am? What more can a driver's license tell me than my age and height and weight, and an address where I once lived?

Opening the wallet to where a driver's license should be, I am relieved. Nothing but business cards, some of them flipped over to reveal notes jotted on the back. In a handwriting that I know is mine. But there is nothing to indicate who I am. How can that be? Has my real wallet been stolen, is this memory loss attributable to a blow on the head? There must be something of me in here. I begin pulling out the cards, reading the notes, little paragraphs and couplets, ideas for stories. I don't remember writing them but they all seem familiar. And I hate that familiarity, I hate this feeling without knowing. I toss the cards to the floor, aware they only flutter to the carpet, they are too lightweight to be flung. And as I release one business card, I realize I have felt something behind it, a different texture, plastic not paper. And there, hidden between cards, is a picture of me, my driver's license, my hair a different color but that face is mine alright. And I feel myself only now waking from the clutter of a dream.

I begin to giggle, knowing this is not how things are but how they could be, knowing I am my own invention.

Keeping the giggles quiet, covering my mouth with my hand, wanting to wake no one. Knowing why I am here. To rid myself of what I am not, what I have become. I am not Sarah Persia.

It is as though I have put myself on a page and now that I am on it, I cannot get off, I am a character in someone else's book. But this book is mine and I cannot help smiling, I am beginning to know what it is I have forgotten. I am a writer, a creator of characters, and for some reason I have hurled myself away from my creative world. Away from me, away for a reason, because the me I have known was in trouble, something had happened to her. She was accused. I was accused. The phone call; Otto was dead. Ms. Malcolm, they greeted me. The press. And not long after, the police, who did not bother to call but came and took me. I was in tears and they took me away, they chose to interpret my grief as guilt. And I was never guilty, not of that. Of too many things, of not being there with him at that moment to protect him, he who never needed protection, who would never have wanted to be saved, who always expected to change the scene himself regardless of who else was in it. I lie awake, shaken, still drunk on this couch. There is no room for anything but grief. Which is part of life. Which is what I had gotten away from, unable to protect him, then desperately trying to protect myself.

Woke up on stomach, diagnosis: must have been drunk. Don't let her die choking on her own vomit, so sayeth the merciful host. The other kind throws body on street and disavows knowledge.

Get up, shake off blanket, shoes already on, stand. Unfold body, fold blanket. Pick up cards from floor, drop into purse. This will have to do as thanks, whether or not sufficient.

End is here, room not bright but too bright. Alone. "My name," I say quietly, feeling my body quiver, "is Sherilee Malcolm."

No answer, no sound at all, not even echo. My legs straighten. "My name," I say at normal volume, "is Sherilee Malcolm."

Distance, something, not in this room. Footsteps approach. "Name," I say, voice dropping once more, "Sherilee Malcolm."

In small living room, familiar now, in spite of emptiness. Door opens. Two shapes, human, male and female.

"My name!" I scream, "Is Sherilee Malcolm! My name is Sherilee Malcolm! MY NAME IS SHERILEE MALCOLM!"

Two run, grab, hold down. Laugh, laugh, laugh; they say hush, other such platitudes. Snarl, growl, bark, howl. Good howl.

"It's okay," they say, "take it easy, it's alright."

Yeah, yeah, yeah, fucking experts. "No!" I scream. "No! No! No!"

Lash out with both arms, knock them aside, bolt upward and away.

"I am Sherilee Malcolm!" I shriek, running out into hall, through front door and into comforts of strange morning street.

———

At home I search for my necklace, search for my ring. Things are lost, remind me of other things I'd forgotten I had, can't find them either. Maybe my cover's blown, and my matching accessories too. And what of the potential friends and lovers I've met and that's about all? Will they also be left behind? I don't know, but I'm tired of being a blonde.

One last time I dress the part of the struggling writer who can't write, who sits in cafés and talks about art, who makes scenes in bars and at parties as though that had never been done. This morning I walked into the world as a blonde, but by evening my dark self will return. I will go out now and purchase supplies, fuel for the flame that must rise once more. No mere ember, no mere flicker of dying light and heat, but a source of uncontrollable burning, a torch for shadowed lovers, emanating smoke that chokes all who oppose us. Theirs is a world without mercy and ours is a world of nothing but ice, decreeing that beauty is there for those who create it, and so is love and hate and pain. Yes there are horrors in this world and we must somehow fight them, and that fight will not take place while wallowing in self-pity; surrender is a moment

I have given up on. Tonight I will once again wear my hair black, tonight I will dress the way I want to dress, and parade through this city like I own it. No more bowing down to others or even to my fears. I fear no man, the Black Widow walks, nothing is beneath my contempt. Into my parlor with all of you; it's feeding time.

I entered Zim's with a smile. The morning felt slow and lazy, the percentage of people looking like artists was remarkably low, the coffee would be bad, the world was perfect.

Ordering, I caught out the corner of one eye a strange grin on the face of a tall, broad man to my left. He looked about my age, wore a rumpled white shirt and black slacks. He raised himself from his chair and lifted his cup. Oh great, I thought. I've tried to pay one last anonymous, quiet visit to middle America, forgetting what I think of it. The joys of a normal coffee shop, where the truck stop comes to the big city.

The lug settled in beside me. "Hello," he said, his smile widening. "I should have known you'd be blonde."

"Am I supposed to know you?"

"We've never met," he said, "but I'm afraid I'd know you anywhere. Under any circumstances."

He held out his hand for me to shake.

"The name is Wash Shank."

It was a strange name, but his claiming to know me struck me as stranger. "And I—"

"No alias necessary, any will do. May I call you Sherilee?"

BOOK TWO

CHAPTER 1
SHERILEE/WASH

She admitted her name but revealed little else. And Wash was so surprised to find Sherilee Malcolm across a cheap diner table that the questions he'd had for her since the time of her trial came no closer to his lips than did any other swarm of alien words. Here was this woman he had admired for years, and been attracted to, and now he was with her, admiration and desire overwhelming any doubts. The things he had needed to know seemed trivial in her presence. Each moment had to be taken as its own, this one to be cherished. Those questions could arise later, like serpents.

For the time being it was enough to sit with her, to drink coffee, to lightly touch on his having been her employee, and for her to respond that she didn't know who the lawyers hired, she only knew who hired the lawyers. And they'd been paid to get her off. A small smile flashed across her face.

Wash's hand reached across the table and squeezed Sherilee's. He let go, then jerked his hand back to his side of the table, shook his head and smiled weakly to himself.

The smile Sherilee returned seemed pensive, not the practiced condescending grin he would expect from her but genuine, appreciative. She extended her arm and gave his retreating hand a reciprocal squeeze, made sure his eyes met hers before she relinquished her grip.

They finished their coffees under a mask of calm. But when their cups were empty all they had was each other, no more distracting props, and the calm, the sense of ease, drifted, leaving a discomfort punctuated only by talk too small to mention, but seemingly necessary. Forced words.

Wash was used to controlling conversations, but those were with people he felt smarter than, superior to. Here he was with Sherilee Malcolm, her name reverberating in his head, and maybe she had survived enough Hell without him putting her through more. And even though he did not intend to put her through any now, he would at some point be compelled to know more about her than she wanted to have known. His usual displayed reserve would have to overpower the nerves tightening like a fist in his chest, aching to slam through.

She looked at him as though he were expected, perhaps even a relief, as after her three years in hiding he must have been. And to be recognized, if this was the first time, within hours of the time she had chosen to be seen.

Perhaps she had been so easy to see because, although still in costume, she again sat with the assurance of being Sherilee Malcolm—a sense of control, an essential part of her that had only recently returned.

That her façades were less obvious than his came as no surprise. Her reputation had been built on the disguising of the false as true. Whereas his work entailed becoming privy to the thoughts of a stranger, then causing the stranger to change those thoughts. He helped people alter their beliefs, helped them to see what the clients needed seen.

It was like magic, the transformation a witness's testimony would take after a talk with Wash. He didn't resort to strong-arm, yet he could make a person say almost anything. But this Sherilee, unlike the loquacious one of her younger days, seemed to embrace silence, gave little away.

Words disappeared, replaced by looks, small gestures, glances brief or prolonged. The two of them slouched and smiled, shrugged and stood, paid their tabs and made their exit. Unable to let her out of his sight, he would drive her home.

Yet he watched her as little as he could while he drove, his eyes fixing themselves on the road, and the mirrors, and the dash. He had to treat her as he treated any interview, he had to regain his habitual control. To find out who she was by acting as she acted. If she intended to reveal nothing then he would have to be alert to every nuance, attuned to the subtly pivotal.

Sherilee would not speak, Wash would not speak, in that there would be no difference between them, and all other differences should stand out. But only if he could read them. In their silence they had to come together, not apart.

As in driving the car becomes an extension of the driver, and in shooting the gun an extension of the shooter, Wash had to immerse himself in Sherilee, to make *her* an extension of *him*. The immersion was the difficult part. Manipulating her afterward would be a cakewalk.

The small Spanish-style house Sherilee called home did not surprise Wash, nor did the little bedroom, with bath down the hall. Especially after she explained that it was a short-term housesitting gig. He was familiar with austerity in times of crisis, the elimination of unnecessary appendages in an attempt to discover self. Solitude, isolation, a black room. But this black was only an impression, not something actually there; the walls were pale blue, a sadness not Sherilee's.

Hers was a bleakness lifting, mourning incomplete, but tears shed, veil gone. The dead remain dead; the living must wait their turn.

She had stepped into the bedroom and he had stepped in behind her, drawing from her the question of what he was planning to do.

He shrugged, walked around the room whistling a light tune,

becoming comfortable here, looked out the window and decided she wouldn't jump to escape him.

"I guess I'll let you get dressed," he said.

"That isn't what I'm doing yet. My hair comes first. You're welcome to wait. In the living room."

Wash stepped into the hall, looked Sherilee's bedroom door up and down. "I could pick this lock in seconds if I wanted."

Opening a dresser drawer and removing two towels, Sherilee looked Wash in the eye and stepped toward him, drugstore bag still in her hand. "I suppose you could."

They both stepped out of the room and toward their immediate destinations.

Wash sat on a comfortably lumpy living room couch. He closed his eyes, threw back his thick arms and rested them along the top of the couch. He thought that now would be a good time to change his clothes, while she got ready, but that would only kill a minute, he'd save it for when a minute might seem like it mattered. Now he had at least an hour, and he needed to find something to fill more of that time.

The virtual invitation to search Sherilee's room had been only that, virtual, and it was her view of his virtue that was likely to be lost if he were to search the room and somehow give himself away. And he sensed that, with her, he would. She had made it easier for him to get into her room, and that made it harder. Of course, if it was what he had planned on doing he wouldn't have mentioned the ease of popping the lock.

What he wanted to find out from her was personal, and he might not need his usual methods. If he liked what he discovered he might never need to alienate her. But he had to use some of those methods because he had to be effective, he had to know.

He felt oddly responsible for the change in Simon Parker. He had to find out what had happened to other people. A woman's life had been saved, and seeing her today, Wash was certain her life had been worth saving, he was certain of her innocence. But what was that innocence worth, how much of how many lives? These were questions that had not occurred to Wash during the case, that may have never occurred to him if he had not seen Simon Parker again. And he wondered about other cases he had handled, witnesses he had maneuvered and never seen again. But if the maneuvering was the problem, could he maneuver Sherilee now?

He shook his tipped-back head, opened his eyes halfway, looked at the ceiling and the specks of dust that fluttered beneath it. He had no answers, only questions, and Sherilee Malcolm would have to answer all she could. Circumstances no longer allowed her even a modicum of innocence.

Not that he could judge her (although he would) but that he had to know the lengths to which everyone else was involved, to see how he fit in, in order to judge himself.

He knew that "following orders" was a Nazi defense, but also that following orders was what most people did, and it was his own morality, intelligence, and gullibility he was choosing to judge.

Wash smiled in his languor. Again his eyes were closed. Blonde hair to black, that didn't seem possible in an hour or so. He smiled. She'd been wearing a wig, and he hadn't noticed. Fucking great detective. It wasn't what he was looking for, so he hadn't seen it. Exactly the sort of thing he had to see. He had to see this woman, not the image she presented.

She at least had a past she wished to return to. The more he learned about his the more he regretted having been there once. And Sherilee Malcolm? Only now, he supposed, was she burying her dead. Only now could she carve out a future. And she needed pieces of her past as an anchor, to prevent her from drifting once more.

CHAPTER 2
SHERILEE/WASH

IN THE MIRROR HER CLEAN FACE SMILED, HER ONCE AGAIN BLACK hair hung down her naked body, almost white, thin—not weak —but no longer holding the strength it once had. Physical strength, she thought once more and hoped. Mentally, she was only now getting there. That fine age again where everything she had written before was garbage, better than most garbage perhaps, but only on a scale of crap. She reached down and touched her skin, still soft where it was supposed to be, if not so soft as it had once been, her eyes on the dark eyes in the mirror, convinced they had not darkened; it was only the world.

Wash was in the bathroom down the hall—for him a change of clothes was simple, he kept one suit in the trunk of his car— and there were no options for her either, except to live or not to live (catchy, that) and now she was allowing herself to be tripped up by this trivial decision of what to wear.

She had to feel streamlined, she had to fly high, she had to take over. And why? Not to show that she hadn't been hurt, but to show she had gotten through it. So, did she want the flashy show she would have put on years before, or should she let the city come back to her?

She smiled, without a glance in the mirror over her dresser. She had new friends she should be introduced to. Thank you, Sarah Persia.

Sherilee Malcolm dressed in black, comfortably tight jeans and sweater, and dropped a circle of plastic Mardi Gras beads around her neck. This was well-dressed by her standards, nothing expensive and all of it looked good on her; the world she ruled was not one that spent much time shopping.

It was only a question of shoes she could enjoy all night. Not comfort but, if she were to look down, pleasure.

She kicked Sarah's already scuffed black sneakers underneath the bed, opened her closet and scanned the floor. This was the least of her worries, but for now the last; she could spend eternity on it.

Or she could grab those snakeskin boots from the corner and be done with it.

She did, and she was. She sat on the bed, crossed her legs, looked at her boots, and wolf whistled. She lay back a minute and waited, for that moment when she would have to rise.

The old but well-maintained Buick gave the pair a smooth ride, from Mission Dolores into the Mission proper. They would be better dressed than most of the other barhoppers on this side of town, with a different purpose. Nothing so simple as sex, or even sexual love. This was a return, if not from her own grave then at least from the unknown.

The drive was brief and so were their words: Wash asked where they were going and Sherilee told him.

"The murder of Otto Workman," a phrase still dominant in Sherilee's mind, could not make it through her lips. She did not know how to complete the sentence, what the remainder of the thought could be.

She told Wash where to turn and he did, and when they were close enough to look for parking he slowed, rooted around.

This was it, Sherilee knew, unsnapping her seatbelt three blocks away from Doctor B's and Christine. She stood on the sidewalk stretching her legs, waited for Wash, this man she didn't know—seemingly kind but with an air of danger—to get out of the car.

The street was dark but it hadn't been for long, and the weak bulbs on some corners kept enough light between open bars, restaurants, and bookstores for all but the terminally lost to find their way. And those people here dead or dying or both, their words disintegrating into words that might have been, sunglasses worn like pennies gleaming in the dark, their lives screaming, staggering, or sauntering, internally vacant or over-flowing, bodies caught between, idling passage into and through the endless hope of night, truth beauty paradise different for each one, every word different for each one.

Wash by her side or behind her steady pace, Sherilee walked past them all, knowing she was nervous even while believing she would be accepted, and her disguise would be understood. She wasn't really different from what she had pretended, far worse lies had been forgiven. It all depended on what you meant by lies.

Doctor B's. The sign shone in the dark. Sherilee stopped beneath it, and Wash stopped with her. She took a deep breath, exhaled and stepped forward. Returning to a place Sherilee had never been.

Going back to Christine, she thought, walking through the open door and into an elbow. She hadn't seen or expected anything like this mass of people, was taken aback by the roaring music, had never been here at this time of night.

And this Christine she so looked forward to seeing was a woman she had met only once. But there had been an affinity, a kinship. Sherilee shuddered, partly in anticipation of rejection, partly in delight. She would have to make her own path through a mob that might not know her.

Moving sideways, bare elbows ready to plunk into the ribs of anyone pushing too hard, Sherilee wedged between bodies and toward the bar. Sherilee Malcolm liked loud music, she liked crowds, she had been away. And now she was back. Smiling but only a moment, pinching her way through cracks, at last she saw an opening between two stools and leaned into the gap. Drawing breath, Sherilee saw a tall, blond man working this side of the bar, and Christine down the opposite end.

It was too loud to holler, Christine would never hear her across this distance. Nor did her eyes drift in this direction. Sherilee smiled, waited for the tall blond to approach. Seeing Wash behind her she extended the smile to him, and asked what he was drinking.

Sherilee explained they were on the wrong side of the room; Wash had already seen. When their drinks arrived he took one in his left hand and put his right around her narrow shoulders, guided her as he gracefully muscled his way into the rabble.

This new route may not have been any quicker but it was more pleasant, knowing now that the moment was upon her, and that Wash was with her in a manner stronger than she'd realized. The room as claustrophobic but the air no longer thin, they squeezed fluidly through the crevices.

When Wash turned his shoulder, Sherilee stepped in front of him, as though they'd been dancing for years.

And there stood Christine, as beautiful as before, her hands in never wasted motion, setting down fresh glasses and pulling away old ones.

Sherilee smiled, took a drink, and smiled again. Christine caught the second smile and returned it, casually, without recognition.

It took Sherilee a minute to realize her drink was too full, that not knowing who she was Christine had no reason to talk to her.

And she had half a busy bar to work; Sherilee's opportune moment was gone.

Quietly cursing her own stupidity, then admiring the easy grace of Christine walking away, Sherilee drank some more, with greater speed. As she set down her finished drink an arm came down alongside hers, and Wash's empty glass touched the bar at the same time as her own.

Christine was busy, taking orders, delivering orders, taking money, making drinks. This would not be the ideal time to talk. But she stepped toward their empty glasses, and it was time for something to be said.

Before Christine could ask what they wanted Sherilee said her name, the real one, extended her hand in greeting, explained how they had met before and watched the surprise on the bartender's face, an acknowledgment of Sherilee's fame that was certain to affect their friendship. Sherilee stumbled on, and Christine's face quickly regained its prior demeanor, but with a brighter smile, and she took the drink order, because she really didn't have time for conversation.

Sherilee and Wash drank slowly, but the rampage at the bar continued unabated, and it seemed best to talk to Christine later.

Somewhere out there were those others she wished to see again. Somewhere she had a number for Ron, somewhere if she'd remembered to get it an address for Jean. She was in the right neighborhood but the odds were against her for a chance meeting on a Friday night. Bars packed with predators rolling dice; would the others on the block be any less crowded, any more hopeful? With a wave to Christine, Sherilee stepped away from the bar, and Wash stepped with her. Anything was better than drinking slowly.

But she did not want a night of mere drunkenness, those had and would come all too often. Stopping for quick shots at the two nearest bars, scanning the faces of compacted multitudes, she found neither salvation nor consolation, only drinks and cigarettes. And thought she might settle for recognition, in a 16th

Street bookstore that stayed open late, where poets of local fame sometimes dropped by to chat with the employees.

And she would be greeted as one of those poets, the prodigal daughter returned.

Brisk winds brought a comfortable cool to the dark night. Sherilee and Wash strolled the not yet dangerous sidewalk past others who ambled as casually as they.

The bookshop window displayed rare items; Sherilee didn't bother to glance. She pushed the door open and Wash strolled in behind her.

A bearded man in his thirties sat in a wooden chair behind the low desk, chatting amiably with a man and woman who sat several feet across from him, one in the direction of either hand.

When Sherilee and Wash walked in the bearded man looked up, began to nod with a polite smile. The nod froze. The smile held a moment, dropped, and was replaced by one gleaming and broad. His friends turned also, their conversation halted.

The proprietor mumbled a couple of words, shook his head, clucked his tongue, rose from his chair, all the things he should be doing automatically overlapping and stumbling over each other. But his face did not redden, his smile remained, he extended his hand in greeting and with a grateful smile of her own Sherilee took it.

At last: to be seen, to be known, to be liked.

Introductions were made all around, Sherilee taking a seat on the corner of the desk, Wash standing at her shoulder. Sherilee entertained with tales of her travels to old romantic lands, as seen by a woman without an acknowledged drop of romance inside her. At the time she'd mocked the places; now she mocked herself.

She talked until late, the star to her audience, until it was time for the store to be closed, then the five adjourned to yet another nearby bar, a new setting for Sherilee's continued regaling.

It was different when the throng was partially her own. Being pressed into a tight space became not discomforting but a means of convergence, and those outside the circle were readily ignored. Yet between tales Sherilee's hopeful eyes would wander, seeking one of her lost friends, unwilling to settle for this ease she had found. And somewhat disturbed that, outside of the bookstore, undisguised she went unrecognized. For she was a semi-famous writer, as famous as most writers get. Unlike Otto, who was a celebrity, a standard bearer for a new generation. It wasn't what he wanted to be, but he was. It was what she wanted to be, if only for a few minutes.

She tried to ignore the progressing hours, but she knew that sometime after midnight the bars should be thinning, that it would be time to return to Christine. Yet the assemblage there had been so great, she determined to wait until closer to one o'clock, not wanting her journey to return her to the morass she'd found it essential to leave.

Sherilee shivered in the night air, and Wash put an arm around her, as though the cold were the cause. Sherilee smiled at him in appreciation; he knew it was something else. Knew he knew more than it seemed he could, that in watching her he was not only absorbed but absorbing. Walking with him she did not need to adjust her stride, he moved in her rhythm. She did not need to watch him to know he smiled back matter-of-factly, that he would be there if she needed protection and as gladly if she did not. It was as though they had done all this before. With only the barest pause, Sherilee resumed her fabling, finished her story as the quintet entered Doctor B's.

Although many people remained, the route to the bar was now direct, and those still here lacked the earlier sense of urgency; they had settled in.

Christine stepped immediately toward Sherilee, and their hands were soon joined. Exuberant eyes flashed on each other and greetings flew forth, as though they knew each other far better than they did, and their last long conversation had been years ago instead of days.

Wash and the others stood back but not far. Although not a part of the excitement, they were peripherally attached. At this hour the customers' needs had slowed down, and Christine could linger a bit.

But the bar, Wash noted with a glance at the clock, would be closing in less than an hour. There would, of course, be time to return, but if they were to continue drinking after that, they should hit a liquor store soon. Requests, anyone?

CHAPTER 3
WASH/SHERILEE

WASH STOOD IN CHRISTINE'S BATHROOM, AWAY FROM SHERILEE AND her bar crowd in the living room. There was no fear in their adrenaline and that gave them pleasure, a calm Wash could never feel on his own. He was trying to sense who Sherilee was and what she was after, and who he was and what he should be after, but all that he saw for himself was a discovery of guilt and liability, and who might escape those with the excuse of ignorance, and who might be blamed with that same excuse. And where mercy came in, if it ever did.

His work was not the noble thing he had once dreamed it could be but only an excuse for acts of cruelty...It was not that simple, there were those he delivered from their troubles, but at what cost to others, at what cost to himself?

He remembered when he worked on Simon Parker, and how far into that head he'd had to go. Parker the witness, whose certainty it had been his job to dislodge. And to do that he'd had to enter Parker's world, the cramped rectangular living room of his small apartment, and gaze upon a wilderness of paintings, a world in which art's primary purpose seemed to be to cause claustrophobia.

This was the world of the artist, as Parker saw it and as Wash had had to see it, to feel what Parker felt, to change what Parker thought he had seen. And he had changed it, removing from Parker's description of the killer not only the certainty but all definition, making the witness doubt his senses, changing the young man's long strides and insistent voice into a stagger and a stammer.

Temporarily submerged in Parker's indistinct world, Wash had rendered both witness and himself useless, uncertain, lost in a haze he had created.

And now recollections of those futile times, his mind in disrepair, the feels and smells of paint on his hands, the dragging minutes he had spent trying to scrub them back to what they had been. And the pointlessness of it, odors and textures returning even before he woke. But he had recovered from that.

He had always been able to find his way into the feelings of others, but his was a mercenary empathy. He did not give a damn about the people he became, he only understood them.

There were things people had to have, frailties that connected them with others: some form of love. He had yet to find anyone who had only a small such need. However well-hidden or oddly placed that need may have been, once uncovered it was always vast, at times so suddenly obvious it appeared all-encompassing.

With Simon Parker it had been a need to be believed, so he could believe in himself. With Sherilee it was more the usual sort of depleted identity, needing love to again become herself, to regain something she had lost. Maybe she was not so different from Simon after all.

Wash flushed the toilet and ran water from the tap, narrowly refrained from thrusting his hands into it, remembered scrubbing relentlessly, remembered working clay into the shape of Simon Parker's head, remembered the ghastly bust he had molded of himself, knowing it was something Simon would do, would have to do, recreating the man he believed had brought him down, and Wash remembered sculpting the beginnings of Sherilee Malcolm's face and being unable to finish it, remembered without knowing if there was anything to remember.

This time there was nothing to wash off, he had come into this room only for privacy. His thoughts hadn't fit into the living room conversation, he'd been unable to speak them, and unable to stop them. He'd had to step away, to separate what was inside him from what was outside. He couldn't let the others know what he was doing. He watched the water run.

His past wouldn't go away, that wasn't what he was trying to make it do, but before he could talk to people about it he had to make the words coherent. They had to come out from where they were tangled inside him, they had to take a different form. They had to become something he knew how to talk about. And they hadn't done that yet, but now at least he had put some of it into words, and maybe later he would put it on paper; after that it might become something he could say. For now he felt he could push it aside, and listen to someone else's words, or pretend to.

Wash shut off the tap, ran a towel across his dry hands, and returned to Christine's living room, where the others sat as though nothing had happened. Ever.

Drinking casually and talking lightly.

Wash filled his empty glass with scotch and slugged it back, filled it again and grasped it with both hands, then slunk into his corner of the couch.

And somewhere he felt he was indeed living a portion of Sherilee's life. But not a portion she was living now. He could not rise to meet her without first falling as far as she had.

Conversation did its best to outlast the alcohol, but Wash had bought too much. It was required for their celebration and his desolation, and the serene silence that set in shortly after sunrise was more of exhaustion than of completion.

It was time for coffee or sleep. Although at opposite emotional ends, Sherilee and Wash were the only ones who opted for the former. It was too early for anywhere popular or hip, but Wash was an expert on coffee shops open at dawn and had no difficulty finding a nearby breakfast joint that would do admirably. Where eggs fried in too much butter would force strength on his alcohol coated stomach, ready or not.

They sat across from each other at a small table. He was surprised to be with her again, to have spent the night together. They hadn't even kissed, but in a way this was better. If he didn't touch her, nothing could go wrong, he would always have her.

As pleased as he was, and as used to staying up all night as he had become, he could feel the bags under his eyes, bags he was too young for, the weight of his skull tipping forward, and he could see nothing of that in Sherilee, whose 6 a.m. energy so reminded him of some perky young movie ingénue he nearly spit his bacon out one side of his mouth.

He shook his head, amused but despondent. He had been in synch with her and fallen out, into something he felt she must once have been, but certainly was not now. They sipped their coffees simultaneously, but where she swam he floundered, nearly drowned. And no one would save him but himself, although he knew somehow it would be her.

He did not understand, his own thoughts betrayed him, tears filled his eyes. But she had already lived this, and could not live it twice. He pushed himself up from his chair, stood shakily, threw some money on the table, turned his back on her, and walked away.

CHAPTER 4
SHERILEE

SHERILEE FINISHED HER MEAL SLOWLY. SHE WORRIED FOR WASH, BUT his problems were not hers. She did not even know him, what she liked about him was no more than an impression. And maybe that was part of what she liked, that they had barely spoken, that she perceived in him a strength she could not know was there, that perhaps was not.

It was Saturday morning and her legs were stiff, and after a long walk it would be late enough to start trying the cafés where she might find Ron. He was the only person to whom she had spoken much recently, the person from whom she had kept the most.

The one she had told the most, but always from a distance, always doing a dance. Now he could learn her reasons, why she'd had to talk to him without quite telling him; now he could paint her. If she could find him.

If she could not, her body could use the rest, she could go home and sleep, she could find Ron later. But she wanted him to be among the first to know, she would prefer to apprise friends before strangers.

Yet, it was daylight and she was in public, and if she were

seen she were seen. Better, still, to be known. The public that might want her back she did not object to, but they would always greet a persona and a persona would always respond, not a character attempting to disclose itself but one perfectly happy in its disguise.

Certainly she was someone different for everyone she saw, but with someone she liked she was a person who gave, who revealed, who sought and discovered; with an audience she entertained, and any giving or taking was incidental. Her art was left on the page, the rest was reality or publicity.

She got up from the breakfast table refreshed, smiled with the knowledge that the night would wear on her before the morning was out. Alone but herself, she left a sizable tip and blew the waitress a kiss, sprightly sauntered out the door, her hips shifting gaily.

Down the sleeping Castro to Church Street and back into the Mission, where she might even find Ron. And then she remembered; hell, she had a date with him. Alone on the sidewalk, Sherilee laughed. That certainly simplified where to look, if she could only remember when. Oh well, she'd get there early, the shape she was in she could drink more coffee than any woman alive.

———

The words ready to erupt from her when she saw Ron walk in the door were overrun by a higher strain of adrenaline. She ran to him, wrapped her arms around his back as he froze, struggled to speak.

In silence she held him and he held tight to this black-haired woman with the familiar face. The hug ended and they linked arms, Ron bought a coffee to go and together they left the café.

In Ron's studio Sherilee would not sit down, and Ron did not ask her to. She paced, she stood, straight or with a hip jutting out, bent forward hands on knees, rolling a cigarette between her fingers but never lighting it. Ron painted.

His brows tight and lips curving in on each other, pressing together, he would relax only long enough for brief sips from the tall paper cup. Sherilee moved, not speaking, and Ron's brush moved with her.

She had told her stories all night; now she would walk them off, burn them away, empty herself of that unburdening. For there is a time to carry a burden, to flex it, to revel in it.

And a time to portray it, but how?

Ron painted, Sherilee mulled. Then Ron mulled her mulling and painted some more.

For hours this went on, without stop, although Sherilee felt herself drooping. She could also feel Ron's intensity, his need to finish, and it would have been a violation of her beliefs to betray that need. So she continued, even with the thought that her presence might no longer be necessary, that by now Ron had her where he needed her to be. The thing was, it was also where she needed to be.

There were no breaks for food, or drinks, nothing to interrupt except when she had to use the toilet; all else had been superseded. An act of creation was taking place, a portrayal of a vision. Nothing greater could be done, not by these two people, not at this moment.

Ron paused, stepped back, glared at the canvas, stared at Sherilee, lowered his painting hand, his eyes riveted one place but then another. And the hand raised itself, returning brush to canvas, altering what had been, searching for what is, what remains.

Countless times he stopped this way, and always he continued but once. And his fingers came apart from that brush, dropped it to the floor, and he stepped toward Sherilee and she toward him, until again their arms were linked, and he was bringing her back to see, and she saw and was no longer tired, and her doubts about this man were gone: there she was shadows and all. The beauty and the vain and the ugly, he had caught them, and now she wrapped him in her arms, and Ron and Sherilee kissed, stood for the longest time before grappling, laughing, to the floor. Through an open window shade, the light had dimmed, dusk had come. The day was over.

CHAPTER 5
WASH

WASH IN REPOSE, DRINKING A BEER AND WRITING. HE KNEW WHY HE had to do this, he was connecting with his subject and she was a writer, and he knew by the strength of the compulsion the connection was partially made, but he did not see why he seemed to be fighting demons, it had never been like this before. Years of connecting this way, of adopting identities…was there something wrong with Sherilee, something more wrong than with any previous subject? Or had he this one time fallen into the sickest part of a personality, was it a little run of bad luck? Whatever it was, this lack of sleep was unlikely to help, but he was in the grips of an alertness he could not escape. Perhaps he should change the color of his hair.

He smiled, he stood, he wondered what to do. At least there was no casework this weekend, he'd conveniently wrapped things up late Friday afternoon. Timing was everything, he thought, pretending he had it. The smile had lapsed and now it returned. Doom this was not. Only an inability to face something, and an ignorance of what that was.

Slowing things down, he leaned both hands on the table and took two deep breaths. Relaxation might be unattainable, but at least the strain could be lessened. Until he knew what it was for.

He swatted the bottle on the table and watched it flip down to the hardwood floor. Nothing spilled, it was an empty. Once more he smiled. He wasn't insane *yet*.

He knew he had to find Alice and Simon again, to settle the things he'd left open, and he knew it wouldn't be hard to do, it was the sort of thing he did for a living. And of course that was part of the problem, how he earned his money, but he was good at his job and wasn't about to quit.

It wasn't finding Alice and Simon that would be difficult, it was confronting them. About personal matters, not about a job. He kicked the bottle toward the wall and crossed the open floor to the bathroom, where he grabbed a pair of scissors and began to cut his hair.

When it was so short it looked like he was ready for two or three different types of brain surgery, he grabbed a baseball cap and put on some shoes and went looking for a barber who'd shave his head.

Scalped, Wash sat in the chair a moment, pleased with himself, then stood and paid the man. He ran one hand over his tired face, felt the beginnings of loosening flesh on his cheeks, perhaps befitting a man of his age. Certainly it was a recent acquisition, a sign of growing old. Which he thought he was too young to be doing.

Chilled by a breeze sweeping across his new unveiling, Wash smiled and shook his naked head, amused that his neurosis had sent him stumbling into fashion. For on Lower Haight he knew, and after dark South of Market as well, baldness by choice was the only men's hairstyle that dared compete with the ever popular long hair. There were those with hair of lengths between, of course, but they were not men of fashion. Wash chuckled to himself, embarrassed at the way he was thinking, afraid if he continued he might begin cataloguing all the smaller trends in men's hair he'd thus far neglected, and upon completion of that task, proceed to the various ways they dressed. Ugh. For a carnivorous mind to sink so low…

He wore an old T-shirt and black jeans and tennis shoes, having left his cap in the car, the faster to horrify the barber into action. And tired as he was, his feet led him not in the direction of his Buick but toward The Toronado, where a beer or two might level him off, poison to counter the madness.

He sat and he sipped, knew he should sleep, knew he should find Simon, knew he had to find Alice. She was the one he had left because of doubts, because of fears he could not face. And now what he had put behind him was making him turn, was following too close.

He sat at the far end of the bar, where no one could sit behind him, yet there were bathrooms back there. He would hear noises and his neck would swivel. Not that anyone was out to get him, he knew that wasn't it, but he couldn't let anything happen to him, it was up to him to make something happen.

Finishing the pint, leaving the tip, waving off the bartender asking if he wanted another, he stood, weaved slightly after one beer as he crossed the room, a room filled mostly with men, living breathing men, but not the one he sought, the creator of statues, and these were not the statues either, they moved differently, they breathed differently, they did not take his breath, they did not press against him, these people were real, he did not need them.

What he needed was part of Sherilee, part of Simon, part of Alice: the lost part. Like apparitions they beckoned, and somehow he saw, until he was out on the sidewalk, blinded by the sun.

Turning his head, Wash blinked. People were in front of him, but he could hear them behind him. He turned around, and the sound turned with him. Still he was approached from one direction and still he heard only what came from the other.

Wash smiled, saw a gap between cars and ran across the

street. He walked the sidewalk painlessly toward his car, unable to hear individual sounds because there were too many of them, enjoying this undetectability of the raindrop in a flood.

Casually he strolled toward the Buick, knowing this was no more than a bad strange afternoon. He would make it home and he would sleep, and when he woke he would find someone he needed to see, he would at last begin to look.

It was Saturday night when Wash awoke, refreshed but groggy. He stretched in the bed and swung himself out of it, turned on a light to make his way to the kitchen, put on some coffee and picked up the phone.

He was good with numbers and still remembered Alice's, but he was bad with machines, at least when someone human was needed, and he hung up his before hers had completed a sentence. He supposed it was folly to expect to find her home at this hour, but he could not allow his needs to be reduced to realistic expectations.

Setting down the phone, he blinked at the not yet boiling pot of water. Raising the receiver once more to his ear, he punched in that other number, the one that should be easier to call.

But he had nothing to say to Simon, that is, nothing he knew how to say, he was too far into the investigation of Sherilee to even know what he might want from this former subject who had pulled away from him, had ceased to be his, had changed into something not quite fathomable. And where had those statues gone, what was left of the man who had needed to be surrounded by them, but had that need no more?

Simon's phone rang, but that was all, it did not pick up, not even an answering machine. A snag in Wash's attempt to be a man of action. He had abandoned one of the three people he needed to be with, and could not reach the other two. But, he grinned, he knew where they all lived. Only not when they would be home.

Anyway, he had coffee. Or would as soon as he poured it. But to drink it would add artificial energy to his genuine motivations without providing an outlet. Yet there was nothing to do but drink it, and make his own outlet. Wash drank the coffee as calmly as he could, flexed his fingers against each other between sips, incidentally cracked knuckles.

The decision was simple, its results possibly fruitless. He would proceed to Alice's apartment—he still had the keys to the building, somewhere, not that he would need them on a door like that…He could always buzz, she might let him in, in case she didn't answer he'd leave a note. What he wanted from her was a belief in innocence, not in general but in hers, which would mean a condemnation of how he'd disappeared from her life, a condemnation he felt he deserved even if she was guilty of murder. He hadn't given Alice a chance, and that was its own kind of crime.

When he buzzed from outside she did not answer. The building key in his pocket, he broke in anyway, it fit the way he felt. No one saw him, and what would they have said if they had? He snorted with contempt, sick of other people, glad to ride the elevator alone. And when he reached Alice's apartment door he expected nothing. He knocked. She wouldn't answer, he'd be surprised if she did, if she was home and wanted guests she'd have buzzed him in. She was the only person he wanted to see, and he wasn't even sure what he'd say to her. The door didn't open, there wasn't a sound inside, for now his mouth would be spared the trouble of making sense.

To uncap the pen then, and unfold the sheet of paper, and write the note against her door; but what words would he use? He had to see her, to assuage his guilt. He had tried letting the cards fall and walking away without looking at them, only to find that not knowing what the cards were did not prevent them from falling on *him*.

Too many words, thoughts, in his head. He wrote.

Dear Alice,

I'm sorry for going away like I did. Something came up, you have to believe me. I have found Sherilee Malcolm. I can tell you about the rest in person. Call me.

Wash

He read it over, decided it was as good a note as he was going to write, and slid it under the door. He walked down the hall past Simon's apartment, remembered how much Simon liked to walk, and took the elevator down.

Not expecting Alice's call anytime soon, Wash drove South of Market, to that bar they'd drunk in the day they met. He'd forgotten its name but it wasn't hard to find, it was near the financial district and he remembered the street.

The place was fairly crowded but Alice wasn't in it. Wash found a spot to lean against the bar and ordered a beer, looked around for a familiar face, unable to remember any club Alice might have mentioned. Nope, and this was Saturday night, not the same crowd that came rolling in after work Friday. Wash drank his Dos Equis and said nothing to anyone, made eye contact with everyone he could. No recognition, no hints of familiarity.

Finishing his beer he returned his attention to the bartender. This guy, at least, was the same. He even remembered Alice by name, but he didn't know where she hung out when she wasn't here, and as far as he knew no one here tonight was her friend. Her usual group hadn't been in.

Wash had dealt himself this lousy hand and hadn't done anything yet to deserve good luck. He ordered another beer and watched and waited, drank slowly.

She didn't come in. No one he recognized came in. He began talking to strangers, but none of them knew her, at least that was what they said, and if there were liars among them they were good at it.

It wasn't late, but there was nowhere to go where he'd be more likely to find her. It was wait here or go home and wait by the phone, so Wash kept buying beers and talking to useless strangers. Better than standing alone like some loser stranded lover. Which in a way he was, but it would only hurt to be obvious about it.

He drank and watched. He waited and talked. And he listened, but there was nothing worth hearing, no help was coming now. And that was his only problem in finding Alice: wanting her now. For she would be home eventually, she would be at work Monday morning, she would be in this bar some weeknight soon. But Wash had developed an immediate need, by turning his back on Alice for weeks. And whatever it was she may have done.

He drank without hope of achieving anything tonight, and left drunk at closing time without fear of anything happening to him while he drove. He would not get in an accident, he would not be pulled over. The awful things that would happen to him were internal, and had already staked their claim.

The unaccommodating night completed, Wash woke to stultifying late morning. The fog that should have lifted shortly before he rose seemed to have settled somewhere in his eyes. Blinking washed some of the mist away, and the unspectacular pain in his head would not slow him long. It was Sunday morning, hungover Sunday morning, bound by tedium, but this morning his problems were not general, there was something specific he had to wait for. Someone. She had to call. Or he could try to find Simon. He grunted and stretched and shook his head rapidly, forced the pain on himself.

One shower and two cups of coffee later, saddled with more than a morning's worth of resignation, Wash picked up his telephone and pushed numbers. Reluctantly, he remembered them all. He listened as the phone rang once, twice—three times a lady he sneered to himself. On the fifth ring Simon picked up. And Wash put it down, not wanting to hear the voice without seeing the face.

He finished getting dressed, a dark suit complete with black shoes and steel pointed toes, dressed for work including the possibility of kicking. This was a personal matter and unpleasant, and it was best to be prepared for all difficulties. Tomorrow he would be back on the job; today was the time for settling things.

He did not buzz at the door of Simon's building, he opened it with his key and walked in. Up the stairs, where he might see Simon coming down. Although he'd rather see Alice, and she would most likely take the elevator, she was not this morning's mission. It was one job at a time, and he could not permit distractions.

He pounded on Simon's door, as he had done so many weeks before, and waited for the requisite growls and moans from its opposite side.

They came, he waited, and the door tugged open a crack. An eye peeked out, a fragment of cheekbone revealed. Inside the room was gray. The door shut. Wash blinked and waited, but heard no bolts being unbarred, no locks undone. Rather, steadily receding slow, heavy footsteps.

Wash blinked again. Something welled up inside him, and burst. He roared and slammed himself shoulder-first against the door, then kicked it hard twice and slammed once again.

From within, Simon bellowed unintelligible response, and the plodding could be heard returning toward the door. They *were* words that Simon used. As he got close Wash understood them, obscenities and pronouns.

Wash ceased his battering when he heard Simon inside the door, muttering the obscenities now.

All the locks undone, the door once more opened a crack. Not waiting for Simon's rude greeting, Wash again kicked the door as hard as he could. It bounced against Simon and he stepped back off balance. Wash slammed through the gap, hands reached up, throttled Simon's neck, and Wash's body lunged forward, brought the larger man crashing down beneath him.

Choking with one hand, Wash punched with the other. Simon, on his back, lay gasping for breath, Wash pummeling him too rapidly for his surprised victim to respond.

Simon barely this side of conscious, Wash smacked him back and forth open handed, one heavy slap for each question asked, until he was satisfied with Simon's answers, and giddy himself from the joy of the beating.

He left Simon lying on the floor, bleeding out both sides of his mouth, gasping and crying. Wash shut the door, his hangover gone, sweat dripping through his clothes, a silly smile draped across his face.

CHAPTER 6
WASH

WASH PARKED OUTSIDE THE OLD BUILDING, WALKED UP THE FRONT steps and buzzed the number Simon had given him. He waited, straightened his shirt and pulled it flat where it had bunched up in the scuffle. Simon wouldn't have called the cops, not on a personal matter; the police couldn't get his revenge for him. At some point Simon might come to settle things, but Wash wasn't worried about that, even if Simon could find him at his new apartment. What mattered now was Simon had probably gotten off the floor and given his friend a warning call, and it was damn unlikely he'd be buzzed inside.

Wash waited awhile, pressed the bell again, and wasn't surprised when there was still no answer. He realized he had not gotten close enough to Simon before, not close enough to understand the relationship between the man and what he made. Only now, seeing how close Sherilee was to her writing, did Wash comprehend Simon's sacrifice. His hand ran back to sweep through his hair, and he smiled at his forgotten baldness. He supposed he should shop for a hat.

He returned home sporting a gray fedora that set him back more than a reasonable man would be willing to spend. But Wash's baldness was not the result of being a reasonable man, and wearing a nice hat had become more a necessity than an option. There were occasions inappropriate for either bared head or ballcap.

He set the hat on the table where he could admire it while he ate, pulled sandwich fixings from the fridge, and froze with a smile at his message machine's flashing light. He shut the refrigerator door behind him as he leaned toward the machine and pressed its message button.

Alice's voice, not shaky but thin, spoke to Wash as he spread mustard on bread, kept speaking while he sliced the ham and the cheese. She wanted to talk, she wanted to hear what he had to say, she wanted to hear about Sherilee Malcolm.

Wash wasn't surprised she sounded most enthusiastic about the last point; he could not expect any more from her than caution, and would not be surprised by accusations of betrayal. He had, after all, left her alone when she needed support.

He called her back; she was doing nothing. It was Sunday afternoon, everyone was doing nothing. They could get together, and have coffee or something, and talk. She named a place. He could be there in fifteen minutes. He finished his sandwich and put his hat back on.

———

She looked as good as ever, although a bit tired. He was tired too, and nervous. Yet a part of him felt great. He was sorry it didn't seem right to kiss her, and he didn't. But he stood when she walked in, took one of her hands in each of his, ordered her a coffee.

She sat across from him, a short table only, but being so close was what made it so difficult. To put into words. That could come out of his mouth, or hers, he saw, as they sat silently together. Not comfortably. Wanting to talk. To get past the past, but it remained too near.

Admitting they were stuck with what they'd done, even though they couldn't explain. She couldn't be sure what all of it was, and she was still scared of what she didn't remember. He assured her that was alright, he knew her too well for it to be anything.

But he didn't know her, and she didn't know him. And knowing some of what he'd done, she still couldn't understand. How could he have left her when she needed him there? He didn't know. Maybe he was weak about that sort of thing. He was sorry.

And he knew that wasn't enough. But it was all he had right now, he'd make it up to her later. Somehow. He'd stay by her now no matter what. There was a look in her eyes like maybe she doubted that, and he knew that was what common sense would tell her to do.

He had to overcome what he had been. And she had to know what she had been. He didn't know if they could be lovers and do that. Right now, she didn't care. About being lovers. The other part, not knowing what she did in her blackouts, that mattered. And every time she found someone who seemed like he'd help, he disappeared.

Wash lowered his head and stared into his coffee. He wanted to flip the table over and put things right, but one wouldn't do the other. He exhaled harshly through his teeth, head still down, and reached his hands across the table. His fingertips touched hers. Then hands took hands, held tight.

He looked up. She was still there, her eyes fixed on his, and nothing was right. Except for this moment. And even this was only a promise, it could easily be broken.

They sat and looked at each other and they could not turn away, no smiles on their faces nor hope in their eyes, only need. He stroked the backs of her hands with his thumbs, and she began to smile and she began to cry. He could only look at her tears, falling slowly, and he wanted to make them stop but he knew too well who he was to make promises about who he'd be.

His hands opened and slid away from hers. His eyes, blinking, as though he could do some of her crying for her, but their pains were separate.

He asked her if she wanted to go. She nodded her head and wiped her eyes with one of those hands he had been holding. She lifted her coffee cup halfway to her mouth and coughed.

Setting it down, spilling puddles on the saucer, she stood, trembled.

He stood with her, stepped forward and wrapped an arm around her shoulders, turned her to walk beside him. Tears no longer fell from her eyes, but her body shook as she walked. And Wash, trying to hold her steady, realized there was no point. Except to take her elsewhere and let her cry with him alone, he who had earned it.

Wash held Alice tighter and walked her out the door.

She could not prove she'd never murdered anyone, as no one can prove they have never murdered anyone. The difference was she fit the description of one murderer, even if the man who had described her had accused someone else and had since recanted almost every word he'd said.

The second murder, the one for which no body had been found, her accuser had probably been delusional. But in private conversation she had expressed her own doubts. And there was what she knew about Wash that she'd kept from him. But didn't that knowledge of what he did for a living serve in her defense? Would she have admitted such doubts about herself to a detective if she had ever killed anyone?

Of course not. Wash knew Alice had not killed Otto Workman, and the likelihood of a person with such mild neuroses going instantly wacko, even when propelled by tequila, was close to nil. No matter what she said.

Then he walked out on her before for other reasons.

He couldn't talk about those reasons. Not yet. He could only nod his head and say yes, but he couldn't tell her what he was agreeing to, couldn't tell her why he didn't trust her. Instead he told her he was afraid of commitment, they'd gotten too close too fast, and part of him couldn't handle that. But he missed her, he saw he'd made a mistake.

He let the conversation die a minute. Leave it alone, let the subject change itself, let her see the pain he was in and give her the gift of showing mercy. This was a talk far more intense than their little phone call had hinted at, Alice's professed interest about Sherilee Malcolm not cropping up in person. She seemed to want only to be talked to and to be touched. Forgiveness and beyond was available if he managed to not fuck things up.

But he was a detective for chrissake, and he didn't know who'd done these murders. And if the second murder was all in Simon's mind, hadn't he helped put it there? Wasn't he responsible for Alice being accused?

So of course now he held her, he comforted her, he talked to her, and he would not sleep with her, because that might make all that preceded it look like an act.

And he would not investigate the "murders." The first was too old, the second too unlikely that it actually occurred. But he would look into Simon a bit more, in case.

Without seeing Simon, he hoped. Not only because he'd already attacked him once, but because the guy gave him the creeps. There was some connection between them, and Wash hadn't enjoyed the times he'd made it.

He held Alice by the shoulders, then held her lean cheeks gently between his hands and pulled her close. His head tilted down and to the side and his lips brushed against the side of her neck.

It was a long night of reconciliation, of too much talk and no talk.

Each admitted things the other already knew, but they were necessary admissions. Trust: that was what was to be regained here. No, not regained, for they never had it. They'd had the usual amount of trust, as though this game they were used to playing was more important than reality. Implicit trust had to be given before it was earned. There were times when pain would come, that was all. And there were pleasures, and beyond them, something more: an understanding.

That was what Wash and Alice sought now, with their effusiveness and with their silence. Acceptance of fears and hates and loves and petty grievances, willingness to be engulfed in bad habits. To be engulfed.

Wash found it difficult not to hold Alice, so again he held her. It was a desperation he felt, but not a sad one. This was how life was supposed to be. This felt like love, and if it wasn't, it was at least an opportunity. And if the feeling didn't last, they'd still have this moment.

The worry, the caring, the need, the desire to collapse: the faith that if one fell, the other would catch.

There was no need to smile, no need to talk, no need to touch. Only a need to look at each other. And when that need was gone, they could turn away. And they would no longer need to be together, they would know they had each other.

But this last burst of independence seemed a long way away.

CHAPTER 7
SIMON/WASH

SIMON PARKER POINTED AT AN INANIMATE OBJECT AND SMILED, as though in greeting. Getting up from where he sat he approached the thing. If he could touch it, he could control it.

Without naming the object.

We name things, explain them, so others will understand things as we understand them. Thus, Newton. Thus, Rodin.

But these explanations without words are easily misunderstood. And to not understand a man who is your enemy, to not become a part of him, increases the chance that he will make you a victim. To not see all his possibilities reduces the number of ways you can sculpt him. To converse with madmen, that is a possibility of all conversations, madness possible in all creatures.

With one hand Simon lifted the long, rectangular object from its place along the shore, shook the sand from it. Driftwood. He would do something with it, though he didn't know what. For now he would turn his back to the water with it, he would feel the sand around each bare foot as he walked away, slow steps, trying to feel everything. He tried to see everything. It would be a very slow departure, if it was a departure at all, for in another direction it was an approach. Always, he was leaving something behind, and always, he entered something new.

He could not keep up with the changes, no matter what speed he walked. So he would try only to become a part of as much as he could, to let it become a part of him. And to know it.

Many things made him smile now. Sometimes he felt there was choice, sometimes he felt there was destiny, sometimes he felt there was only what he could make with his hands.

Simon worked the wood with a small hatchet, then sawed and planed it, chopped the girl's figure naked, without words, nothing but shape and movement.

He sanded her down and painted those portions needing paint. She was a miniature of someone he had seen once, and now, full as her lips were, his dwarfed hers when they kissed.

Wash waited outside the old building, wanting to get done quickly so he wouldn't be too late for work, waited for Simon's drab little friend. He looked at the photo, lowered it, looked at it again. There'd be no mistaking the young death rocker when he left his home.

When the backward-ballcapped longhair stepped out of his building and strolled leisurely down the street, Wash waited a couple of minutes, in case the menially laboring guitarist had forgotten something. Making sure his own hat was secure, Wash rose stiffly from the car. A man in no hurry, visiting friends.

Like with most of these buildings, the front door was no problem. Not enough break-ins yet for the owner to go to the trouble of making it safe. Wash hurried up the stairs—too many strangers on elevators. The guitarist lived in a second floor loft, and the staircase curled directly to his door. Wash knocked.

The door opened, all the way. The girl was in her early twenties, and she wanted to know who he was. He wanted to know who she was too, but she was the only one who asked.

Now was no time to show surprise. Wash reached inside his jacket and flashed her a badge.

Her lips shaped the letter 'o' and the word popped out in almost silent accompaniment. She stepped back and Wash pushed his way into the room.

She didn't like cops, that wasn't hard to figure, and Wash guessed it was because of the company she kept. Well, there were cops he didn't like either, and for some people it was best if they never saw them, so he wasn't offended by her fear, only bothered that it was directed at him. Not that he was interested in her, but put a pretty woman in front of him and his thoughts always veered that way.

She was a small blonde and she said her name was Mercury and she wanted to know what he wanted, but her demands were defensive and it was easy to turn them on her. He said he'd bust her if she didn't let him in, he could get a warrant later. He knew there was dope in the apartment and didn't care, he was after something else. She asked what, he told her he'd know it when he saw it, she was better off not knowing.

Mercury stepped mincingly backward and Wash stepped in, she could shut the door behind him if she wanted.

The narrow corridor stretched the length of the building. No way the guitarist made the rent on his shitty job, and the girl didn't look high-income either. No wonder she was scared of a cop.

There were little non-rooms along one wall every few yards, one step up and you'd be in a different rectangle. Some were set up like regular rooms except without walls, furniture, places to sit and things to look at. Others were storage spaces, boxes stacked one on top of the other. There was an unmade double bed in the first space, and somewhere there must be a kitchen and a bathroom, but those were details Wash didn't need. He didn't even bother growling 'who else lives here,' it didn't matter, he'd handle them if they showed up. At least one of these little step-up rooms had to contain some of Simon's statues. Wash walked down the corridor, gave each of its raised stages a quick glance.

One of the higher-tiered levels was set up for a band, with amplifiers on either side and room for a drum kit in the back. In another hung a trapeze, hovering several feet above a single mattress. The floor beneath, as in all the rooms, was hardwood.

Down the center of the main room Wash stepped slowly, gazed at dark walls, his eyes longing for the chamber containing the prizes he treasured.

Mercury followed Wash, watched what he watched, wondered what it was he wondered.

But his slow, wordless movements, each cautious advance seeming to sink his foot into the wooden floor, told her nothing. His eyes moved with efficiency, his neck pivoted deliberately.

He knew the frail blonde watched him, and shook slightly. He could feel it, but he could not use those sorts of feelings, they were out of reach right now. His concentration was directed toward shapes in the distance, gargoyles that until this instant had been for him a distant but distinct memory.

They bordered all but the entryway to one of those one-step-up rooms, sculptures along the floor, paintings up and down the back wall extending past the borders of the room to the spaces adjacent. Grotesque caricatures all, but brutal in their realism.

Running or floating, Wash reached the entry to the room, stood there staring, these years later knowing how wrong he'd been when he attributed his initial wariness of these creatures to a sense of claustrophobia. They overwhelmed, but not because of their number or how much space they overflowed. Any one of them could have filled a wall with equal power.

How could the creator of these have loaned them out and never reclaimed them?

Wash realized the girl had said something, and he had not answered, and she was repeating her question.

He shook his head and stepped forward, away from her and up the step, into the space. This was not a moment to be wasted on explanations. So much time had been spent hesitating, when in the depths of his mind he'd known this was where he had to come. All this time, he hadn't been allowing this into him. All this time, it had been there anyway.

The girl uttered words behind him, gibberish. She wanted to know something. All she had to do was look. Simon had somehow given faces to all the little revulsions within Wash, in these fictions created mostly before the two men met. How it could be done Wash did not understand, only that it had been. And that his own little stabs at creation had been acts of dilettantish spite, sculpting to become closer to Simon, writing to become closer to Sherilee.

He stepped into the non-room, looked into eyes that could not be looking back, allowed himself to be surrounded. He felt something and turned. It was a feeling he was not used to. There, on a shelf that had been behind him, a bust stared at his shins. He got down on his knees to face it, saw the face he'd recently been invited to see, the bait Parker had dangled and he had refused.

And now it was here. Its hairline had receded, there were wrinkles on the forehead and under the eyes, chin doubled but cheeks stripped of flesh. The turned-down mouth was opened slightly, revealing sharp yellow teeth with gaps between them. And the eyes barren, but he didn't need to look at them to know that, he could feel their gaze; he didn't need to look but he couldn't turn away. He was staring at himself, and he was so old and ugly he could smell his fetid breath.

Slowly, Wash raised himself from where he squatted, heard the creak of the bones in his legs, backed away with the deliberate steps of an invalid, almost into a wall of gargoyles but he sensed their presence and turned. They were too close for him to see. He stepped back and looked, they were ugly and near, he turned away from them and saw himself again and shuddered.

And the blithering little girl was still saying something, he would send her away if she did not shut up, shut up and admire without being told. There could be no telling, these were not things to be explained.

Tortured by a need to be no one else, feeling what is not supposed to be felt, tormented by the presence of others. Overwhelmed, regardless of how much has been achieved, by how much has not. Afraid life thus far has been lived under false pretenses, attempting to achieve the goals of another man.

And I will never be happy with what would constitute happiness for that other man, when I find that wondrous love he needs I must flee, the greatness I aspire to is something if achieved I must spit on.

Gently dumping the small tubs of paint to form an array of color pools across a vast piece of canvas on the floor, naked Simon dipped, rolled, and splashed himself in the puddles until he felt there were equal amounts of each color on him.

Now he was ready for the other canvas. He flung himself upon it, contorted spasmically, rolled and flopped convulsively. He knew when he had conceived of this that he would look like an idiot doing it, but now he knew no such thing, he knew only to leave the moves to his body and to let it quit when he was done.

Writhing, slamming, rising and diving, Simon bruised himself beneath the paint but he did not stop, he was pounding, arcing, leaping as if to fly. The paint, his body, the canvas. Naked except for paint. He had to continue until he could not continue, he wanted to stop but he could not stop. Roaring as he moved, guttural sounds and the squealing cries of a bird, all that had to escape him would. Until he was done, slumped forward, immobilized by this, this thing he'd found he had to do.

Simon flopped off the canvas, too weak to know if what he had done was any damn good, only that it had been necessary for him, that he would look at it now but might not be able to see it properly. If there was a proper way of seeing it.

Too tired to stand on his own, he was helped to his feet by two gallery employees. Time for the bath. Too weak to wave, he nodded his head to the cheering fans pressing toward him.

Wash wanted to take the girl in his arms and protect her, and make love to her, and own her. Then he would be the one she needed protection from. Maybe that was what she was thinking now. She took two steps away, and he did not raise his arms from his sides. He would not make love to her because he needed someone, or even talk to her because he needed someone. His needs were too many, no one could satisfy them all. Damn few could satisfy any, except momentarily. There was something physical he needed, and something emotional, and whatever any of it was he could not touch it, certainly not by touching her. Or not by touching only her. There was a constant longing, a craving, somehow he needed every woman he wanted to love him one iota differently.

And in that search for himself he would find aspects of each of them, revealing hidden pieces, giving to each woman a part of herself she did not know she had.

He turned away from the sculptures and paintings. They had given him all he could take for now. The girl had shrunk away somewhere, he did not see her.

He wanted to talk to her, although he had nothing to say. And he wanted to take the sculptures and paintings with him, he had to see them again. But Simon would never sell them, not to him.

Wash roamed down the runway, moved quickly and looked for the girl. She had to be here somewhere, she couldn't be hard to find. He tried to remember what she had said when he had not been listening, but there wasn't much he had heard. Something about 'freak.' And he knew she had been referring to him. So maybe she'd bailed, gone straight out the door, thinking he was strange. Hell, he smiled, she was young. Everyone was strange.

He had done what she had done, clung to something that did not exist, in his case a life without pain, in hers a vicarious existence, that of the groupie to the star. If only a small star. Like satellites they both drifted, allowed themselves to be pulled, by gravities of their own creation.

Knowing it was pain he had always dodged, that the dodges had been unsuccessful, that what had been shunted aside had remained always skulking, that all he had done was leave himself unprepared at those moments when the agonies would emerge. He had made himself as he had made others: a victim.

Love made by the ravenous, without need of or time for explanation: Sherilee and Ron gorged themselves on each other, needing something and getting something, and for now it didn't matter if those were the same things.

As though turning away from pain were an answer. Clutching at the body beside hers, and as comfortable as she was with it in motion or inert, as much as she liked the man, it was another man she thought of, whose absence ate away at whatever it was she had inside. Her dreams could not be peaceful for long, nor could her waking moments. She could not forget that a body resembling hers had been responsible for the destruction of Otto's.

She knew she was not as brave as she had pretended, or even as brave as she had thought. But she was braver now than she had been. She did not treasure this added courage that had been forced upon her, she was not enthralled with wonder at how this higher trauma might force itself into and thus broaden the expanse of her writing. She wanted her old limits back.

This was pointless, she could not have them. She had to take what she could. She stroked Ron's bare back. It was smoother than Otto's, did not hold as many knots. She shuddered briefly, draped one long, lean thigh across Ron's ass, stroked his skin with outstretched fingers, began to wake him.

Wash walked the apartment, searched every section, but the girl was gone. He did not wonder where she might have run to, he was not concerned. Likely she was gone from his life, and he didn't suppose it mattered much. He made an earnest about-face, marched steadily back to the place he wished he hadn't left.

There were the statues, there were the paintings. He wished he could take them all with him but he could not. He wished the statue of Sherilee was here, he could take that, but it was not. The statue of himself...he sneered at the ugly bust, it radiated a hate toward him that at the time of its completion he had not yet earned. Not from Simon.

It was a punching bag he needed, and the bust might break his hand, but that vision of loathing was what he had to stare back at. He lifted it with both hands: not too heavy. Toting it like a misshapen football, Wash walked quickly, broke into a jog, then ran full speed with it until he was at the door, past the door, at the stairs and down the stairs, outside and at the car and setting the thing on the street as he flipped frenetically through too damn many keys. Finding the one that fit the lock, he opened the door and bent down, picked up the caricature of himself and laid it on the floor of the passenger seat.

He flopped himself into some semblance of comfort behind the wheel, pushed down on the gas and turned the key, then slid the seatbelt into place. The agency offices were only a short drive across town. Wash pulled away from the curb and headed in the opposite direction, toward the freeway.

Nowhere to go and it didn't matter where he went, he was set to explode and he had to drive. The gray flatbed truck in front of him barely moved, five miles under the speed limit for no goddamn reason. But there wasn't time to pass before the on-ramp.

The truck also pulled onto the on-ramp, and it still didn't accelerate, not so far as he could tell. Almost time to merge onto the freeway and that fucking truck was still doing thirty. He didn't like to tailgate but he didn't have much choice, the blue van on his butt didn't exactly exude patience.

Onto the freeway and a bit of luck, no one in the slow lane. No way to drop further back and shoot around the gray snail but fuck it, no one in the side mirror and the van hadn't moved over yet. Wash flipped on his blinker, hit the gas and pulled into the left lane.

Brakes screeched behind him, horns blared, and he swerved back to where he'd come from. Now it was beside him, he could still hear the brakes, he'd missed getting slammed into from behind. Their cars less than a foot apart.

He shuddered, didn't know where that car came from. The kid in the little white economy model didn't bother to flip him off, straightened out and floored it, got the hell out of there.

Wash settled back into the slow lane, determined not to pass anyone for a while. The gray flatbed was no longer in front of him. He wondered where the bastard had gone, must have taken the first off-ramp. Ah well, he was the bastard now. He might have killed that kid, and if he'd killed himself he'd have deserted

Alice again, after promising not to. He realized this fear of leaving someone else alone disturbed him more than his own mortality. And he couldn't help feeling relieved, somehow the near tragedy eased the tension.

But didn't eliminate it. He'd get off the freeway at the next off-ramp and turn around, take neighborhood streets home, drive slowly. Inside his apartment he would find a place for his new trophy. He drove the speed limit now, not wanting to catch up with anyone, not wanting to be tailgated, wanting to be near no one. He turned off as soon as an off-ramp reached him.

And drove through neighborhoods nice enough for leaving garage doors open, revealing bicycles and barbells, walls graced with glistening tools hanging on unseen hooks, and one car parked snug in its half of the two car garage.

Wash realized as a dead man how little he would be missed, how few he would leave behind. There was Alice, his current lover who barely knew him, who probably didn't know she was his current lover as they'd done virtually nothing. No old girlfriends he'd kept track of, no friends of any kind. And no family. He was close to no one at work; he'd taken a job requiring a solitary approach.

He wouldn't be missed, except by Alice, and even she didn't need him so much as she needed *someone*. He had arrived at the time she was needy, that was all. But it did not need to be all. He did not need to be always alone, as she could not stand to be.

But what about his job, he thought, parking in the tenant lot. That was where he was supposed to be. It was what he had done —had been—for years. And it had to be over now.

* * *

A dresser stood against the wall opposite Wash's bed. Wash placed the bust on it, propped two pillows against the wall at the head of the bed, and leaned back. He stared across the room, faced that face.

He saw himself as Simon had seen him, hated himself as Simon had hated him, and he relished this moment of sheer indulgence. Perhaps no one else could see as you saw, Simon, with vision so beautifully cruelly true, but I am ready now, I will be your audience.

CHAPTER 8
SIMON/WASH/SHERILEE

SIMON HAD AN AUDIENCE. EARNED, OF COURSE, NOT VIA GREAT artistic achievement (although that was a possible sidelight) but with an act of extravagant exhibitionism. It was the means that got people's attention, the end was everywhere. Art inundated the city. The number of self-proclaimed artists per capita had to be among the nation's highest.

But why people watched him was secondary. It was a matter of tricking them into watching when he did something good. Fooling people. It was what everyone else thought they were so good at. It was not what he wanted to do. He wanted to show what people were, peel back their flesh until only their humanity remained. He needed them, those who watched and those he watched, those who saw his work and those who were his work. But he needed them for different reasons, and need wasn't really the right word. They were a convenience, not a necessity.

But that was putting their role too lightly. Without them he could subsist, but he would never flourish. And he had subsisted too long. He hated restaurant work, and factory work, and delivery work. Fuck, he hated *work*. Always working for someone else. It didn't even matter if the money was alright, except then he could spend fewer hours doing it. He saw differently than others, he was sure of it, and he could create what he saw. No one else could create it, no one else could see it.

Simon bathed for hours, soaked away the scent of the paint he loved, readied himself for that next virgin moment, when he would again plunge in. His plan was to create a painting on a large standing canvas then dive through it, destroying one creation while simultaneously revealing others, a mixed media display that would stand hidden behind the canvas. And film the whole thing. It was this other art people needed to see, not the spastic gyrations that bounced him off floors and walls. Although of course those too. It was not that this new form was greater or lesser, but that he was thus far unsure of how much he achieved with it.

He stood up naked in the tub, water draining, grabbed a towel and stepped out. Looking down on himself, he admired the many bruises. If nothing else, this new work had brought him that. Blood purpling flesh. Soon he would have to cut some of it open. Moving on to the next technique.

Wash's phone rang. He did his best not to hear it, and not to hear the message, tried only to return the statue's stare. But his concentration wasn't that strong. He heard the voice—work wanting to know where he was. He ran the warm palm of first one hand then the other over his bare dome. Jobless was what he would be, then he would have to do something else.

But security guard jobs were fucking dreary, and his own private agency would be a bitch to establish. It wasn't like he could refer to the specifics of his odious past. But it felt good thinking of it as past, the implication of a future without it. The realization.

For now it meant facing the present, the shattered fragments of days he couldn't ignore. It meant looking at a face indissolubly hideous, and recognizing it as himself and as normal, that is, nothing was normal but some things were usual. He'd made mistakes and it was too late now to do anything about most of them, but somehow he'd have to repair any visible damage he'd caused.

That was what he was trying to do when he beat up Simon: find those statues, retrieve those memories. It seemed to contradict his aims, hurting Simon again, but, unless something permanent occurred, Wash wasn't concerned with physical injury. It was scarring that held his interest, internal pains deposited too deeply to be removed.

He was scarred. Simon too, but in a different way. And Alice, and Sherilee. He supposed they had each been toughened. In other different ways. Whether that toughness was desirable, or removable, he didn't know.

Sherilee wrote, of a man in a room with a chair and a television, sitting and watching, and the need for the removal of those instruments of spectatorship. She wrote of a woman in a room adjoining, a woman alone, and the door that did not open, and the texture of its wood. Her fingernails scraped the door, like a cat sharpening its claws, but the woman gains no strength from this, no advantage; she is a different animal.

When Alice got off work Wash was there in his car, to take her away. To what he wasn't sure, but not that bar she liked to frequent. A quieter place on another side of town, somewhere where it was harder to park. Wash was comfortable in North Beach, maybe more for what it once was than for what it had become, but some of its history lived on, enough to imagine it a sanctuary for someone in need of escape.

He'd decided to try to make Alice love him, and he would try to love her, without knowing what love was, except it involved things he wasn't used to, kindness and emotional courage and passion. And to make such a strange effort meant finding a familiar refuge, a place where ease would come to him, at least as much as it could. Let the difficulties arise between him and her, not because of an unfamiliar setting.

He took her to Specs, ordered their drinks and walked her to a table. Here there were signs and faces on the walls, and other things—a baseball bat, a deep sea diver's helmet—that jutted out from both the walls and the ceiling, but none of it felt forced. The art of The Beats remained.

The place was almost empty, it hadn't been open long. A group of early arrivals sat at the near end of the bar, their backs to the wall beside the door. Wash recognized some of them but said nothing, he knew no one by name.

And anyway, he was here to be with Alice, without anyone's crowd. There were things he had to tell her. He didn't know what they were. That was what he had to work on, informing her of the things he didn't know himself. How to do that. It would work with her, or it would fail, and if it failed, he would have to find someone else, and do the same thing. His life had been halfass until now. At least, he didn't remember back to when it hadn't been.

He told her of his difficulties, the ones he could explain that weren't confidential. The immoralities of his job and his need to escape that, to embrace something better. He took her hand but for some reason he did not smile, he could not find that, the intimations of a kindly promise he might not be able to keep.

Instead his face stayed solemn, and his words as well, telling Alice of the past he must abandon. Not right away could he tell her of his commitment to her, fearing she would see it as no more than escape, not a separate step beyond it.

They finished their drinks, they could have been anywhere. But Wash might not have told his tale so well in another place. This dim room suited him. He stood and stepped to the bar, ordered another round, while Alice looked at the carefully chosen curiosities that hung from everywhere. There was more coming off them than she could look at, much of it bizarre as though the space itself had a sense of humor, a sense of the absurd.

It was a strangely eclectic room for intimate conversation. But Wash was not distracted. When his eyes left her face they looked nowhere, he saw nothing except what he must tell her.

He returned to the table and set down their drinks. He hesitated; she waited. Wash took a drink. "I don't know how to say this. But I admire you. You're strong, original, sane. You're stable. You might be my way out."

"Out of what?"

"What I'm in. This criminal investigation shit. It's so negative. It's wrecking me."

"I thought your life was better than mine."

"My life?" He affected a laugh. "See, I couldn't even do that natural. No, you have innocence."

"Innocence? Hardly."

"I'm paid to corrupt how people think. Next to that, innocence, yeah."

"I suppose." She glowed to think of it that way. She had so long felt like a piece stuck awkwardly in the puzzle, was surprised to be told that a part of her appeared superior not to her own surroundings but to those of someone else, and of course she felt better to be reminded of what she had almost forgotten existed in herself.

Strength and originality. And sanity, stability. What she was afraid she didn't have, she had more than anyone he knew. A knowledge of who she was, even if it wasn't everything she wanted to be.

But it was easy to say he wasn't happy with the things he'd done, hard to say what he was going to do. He doubted there was any one thing he could stay with. He had to find a life less constricting.

And she knew what he meant. She felt stuck where she was, not knowing how to get out. Because there was nowhere to go.

Then she would have to say what it was she really wanted. But the words would not come. Then some did, crept out, faltering.

"You know, I always wanted to write, but I never had the education."

"You read, right?"

"Yeah, sure. How'd you think I got into Sherilee?"

"Maybe that's the education a writer needs. Not some fucking degree. MFA is motherfucking asshole. You read, you can write."

"I—I guess I gave up. Gave up on writing because making money had to be work."

"There's that. But you could still write."

"But now I answer phones. Making a living…is nothing but death."

"Walk away with me. The only way out might be to go. Neither of us knows where."

CHAPTER 9
WASH/SIMON

WASH KNEW THE AGENCY WOULD FIND HIM WHEN THEY WANTED TO. He wasn't moving anytime soon; avoiding things was what he was avoiding. Besides, if he acted guilty they might have him killed. There was too much he might know. He couldn't quit, and he had.

But he had no desire to implicate them in anything. It would be too much work, even if it wasn't suicidal. Not that he could defend the kind of work they did, the kind of work he'd done, but he wasn't angelic enough to fight them. And he'd lived by their defenses, even believed them. Now he accepted them as another way of looking at things, not a way he could look anymore, but still defensible. It was his own work he could not defend, his own life that required reversing. And not by becoming a martyr. He didn't see what damn good that would do.

Wash and Alice arrived at the house where Sherilee rented a room, but Sherilee was not there. Not that there was an urgency to finding her, except she was someone Alice had long wanted to meet. Right now that seemed reason enough.

She was in none of those 16th Street bars she and Wash had been to a few nights before, nor in neighboring ones Wash and

Alice managed to think of. At least they hadn't driven, they'd expected to get exceedingly drunk, and when they did they took their time before staggering up to Church Street and catching a late bus back to her place, not his, no telling who might be waiting for him there.

He did not always take Alice with him. He tried to tell her even the things he could not put into words but he couldn't explain the importance of Sherilee, feared trying to explain that to her. Afraid something visceral would betray him. Yet knowing that was what he must face. Nightly Wash sought Sherilee in every one of those bars, and nightly did not find her.

He questioned people in the bars, he questioned people in the bookstores. No one gave an answer worth a damn.

Writing. That was what she was doing, but where? Not at what had been her home. Was it his discovery of where she lived that had driven her from it? Her reappearance in the city had been noted in the papers, but she was a writer, not a rock star. Well known, not famous. Although the murder and trial had briefly made her that, it had been four years since the killing. Still, she seemed to have vanished again. And she had claimed she did not want to be hidden.

Simon had seen murder, but not quite. Not well enough to do anything about it. Except that he could record it, make it visually available, put the faces and other body parts on view before the public.

He would recreate the murder of Otto Workman. This would be his defining moment. He had the attention of a few. With this he would have them all.

He knew what Otto Workman's killer looked like, but he hadn't known until he'd said who it was how many women looked like that. In San Francisco alone. He saw them every-where now, not only when looking at Alice, who physically resembled Sherilee, but in every predatory face he saw. And we're all animals, he realized before the mirror, deciding not to shave, not to comb his tousled hair.

Simon could feel his spirits soaring, and he didn't care how many people before him had had thoughts similar to those he held now; what mattered was what he was going to do about his. His gallery show had gone well, they liked him there, it shouldn't take long to put this new idea into form. Especially if he quit his job. He wouldn't need it anymore.

Wash had gotten a man's first name and description, but without access to agency files it was taking a while to find him. What he needed was a last name, although someone had remembered a café Ron often went to on weekends, so if nothing else turned up by Saturday, Wash at least had that. For now, though, it would be another night of bookstore and bar hopping in the Mission.

Two men stood outside the stairway leading down to the BART station. They were dressed too much like Wash, and he knew he wouldn't be getting on any train tonight. He held up his hands as though being robbed, then asked the men what had taken them so long and where they were going.

The answer was less jovial than the question. They nodded back up the street Wash had come down, and stepped toward him. He turned and walked up the sidewalk toward his place, the two men following.

The incline was steep and remained that way for several blocks, but they reached Wash's building quickly and he was ushered into his own apartment.

The front room was large and dark. Wash flicked on the overhead light. "Drinks?"

Two heads shook. Wash shrugged and poured himself a scotch. Might as well make this as pleasant as possible. It would be a standard debriefing, and he might get cuffed around a little, but they wouldn't need to kill him. He hoped.

They wanted to know what he knew about what Simon knew. Wash's one big fuckup, the one that wouldn't die. This had better be routine. But they peppered him with questions, and he didn't know why. He'd taken care of Simon, he'd been one of the best field workers the agency had, and he'd said the case was closed. What was there about Simon now?

The two thugs in suits shoved Wash down into his chair. One produced a folded newspaper and let it fall in Wash's lap. Wash's eyes dropped to look. A fist slammed into his midsection and he crumpled forward. A shove from behind sent him sprawling to the floor. A foot lifted him into the air and dropped him on his belly. Another kick found its mark beneath his rib cage. Gasping for breath and aching with each, Wash saw the open paper shoved before his face. He blinked a few times, took a painful deep breath, propped himself up on his elbows and looked at the paper.

It was one of the local free rags, open to a page on the arts. His eyes zipped through one little item after another, knowing what he must be looking for.

There. Simon was some kind of celebrity, a performance art sensation. Wowing the locals and making the papers. The concern, of course, was he might become famous. Or the wildness of his shows might be a symptom of his going insane, insane enough to talk. And he was someone now who might be listened to. And what if certain words were to slip?

Wash assured his interrogators there was no possibility of such an occurrence, Simon was not concerned with the agency, the grudges he held were personal.

And there were grudges?

Wash told of his assaulting Simon, explained the act's independence from the Malcolm case, said that Simon had only dealt with the agency in order to deal with him, it was a personal matter.

Sounded like Wash had done some damn stupid things.

He didn't deny it, admitted he was having his own problems, but he was fighting his way through them, he had to get away from the job. The things he had to do for the job, they were fine at the time but now he couldn't do them, not anymore, something else was happening.

Sarcastic words responded, and a laugh, and Wash watched, wondered how much he had been like this, thought he had to have been more, remembered Mercury and how she responded when he said he was a cop.

But these men weren't cops, and they weren't killers either. They were dangerous but discreet and astute. They knew the answer they were looking for, and how distant a resemblance to that answer would qualify.

They would beat Wash some more, they had to find a crack of doubt if there was one, and if there was they would kill Wash. Then they would kill Simon.

So Wash was riddled, with questions and blows, never knowing which was coming, never certain there were answers that would save his life.

***

Alice didn't know what Wash was doing when he didn't see her, and two nights in a row seemed too many of them so soon after his vow of loyalty. He claimed he was trying to love her, that he really thought he could, but then this time of his that seemed like it should be spare he was spending somewhere other than with her.

So after work she was back in the bar, figuring he'd know he could find her there if the thought happened to cross his mind. And that talk about quitting their jobs...here she'd given notice, to be with a man who wasn't here. Damned if she knew where he was, and damn her if she didn't want to.

Love. What a load of shit. Especially coming from a man,

especially the kind she'd like. He'd show up desperately crazy about her whenever it was he needed her, then disappear until the next time. She was familiar with the type. Seemed like the only type she *was* familiar with.

Alice got to drinking, and talking with the usuals. Most of them had given up on picking her up by now—she'd been coming here two years—and that made for a simpler evening. The two beside her at the bar were bike messengers, friends of the bartender, and she trusted them, at least in public.

She was well on her way to drunk, talking to them about Wash when he came tottering in. His face was unbruised but he grimaced with each movement, one foot lumbering along after the other.

She started up but he waved her down, his ribs couldn't take a hug.

"A dispute," he said. "Nothing but business. The business I'm getting out of." He said the last bit with a grin that caused him to grimace once more. He ordered a drink and finished it quickly, ordered another, bought one for her and whispered in her ear something about getting the hell out of this joint. She nodded and smiled, and when his hand touched her elbow they finished their drinks and left.

He tried to tell her in the car, but there was too much he didn't want to say. He mentioned as casually as he could that Simon was getting famous, their old friend the artist had become a bit of a performer as well.

She wanted details but all he knew was what he read in the newspaper, and he didn't have the paper with him.

She hadn't meant those, she didn't want those. But he couldn't tell her the details of the night. There were some things it was safer not to know.

They went back to her place, his was a mess. She didn't have a paper. He promised to get her one in the morning. And he couldn't make love to her tonight, his body hurt too much, but he wanted to lie beside her.

He wanted her to know it was only physical if he cringed when they touched.

———

Simon worked in a fervor, rapidly made arrangements with the gallery, although he could not know when the exhibition would be ready. He trusted inspiration and a deadline, he was certain he was doing something now that would be noticed and remembered by more than a cult.

For the exhibition to be complete he would need some of his old sculptures. They were personal, and there was no other way for this story to be told.

He arrived at Richie's building early in the evening, between the end of the guitarist's work day and the beginning of his rehearsals. Simon held a large box, empty except for old newspapers.

Richie was there, but Mercury was gone. She split one day, without a word or a note, without any reason. Richie was sad she was gone, but it wasn't like they were in love, and it wasn't like he didn't know she was flighty. Still, he missed her, and even with her share he'd barely been making rent.

Simon shook his head. He talked sympathetic, but he didn't really give a fuck. Rent breaks, money breaks, they were always a hassle. *He* was doing something important. So he assured Richie he'd find a new roommate, if not a girlfriend. It wasn't like he'd lost a guitar.

Subject safely changed, Simon took it further, back to what he'd been saying over the phone, that he was working on a new show and he needed a few of his old sculptures for it.

Richie led him back to the private gallery. Simon gazed upon his creations, relieved not to hate them. He couldn't do that kind of work anymore, and was pleased to see they were good. Pleased to enjoy what he had done, what he had been. In their absence he had doubted, them and himself. He smiled, knowing the ones he had come for, saw one, grabbed it, wrapped it in newspaper and set it gently in the box.

There were busts of the lawyers, of the judge—he picked them up and wrapped them one by one—of the nightmares, of himself. But…his eyes swept across his creations, back and forth and again. Where was it? He had brought it over two weeks ago, he knew exactly where it should be. The statue of Wash was missing: he had to have it. Mercury was missing, too.

Richie hadn't looked for her, he didn't see the point, if she wanted to go she was free to go. But he knew the kinds of places she liked, they were the same ones he did. Clubs and cafés, and she sometimes took long walks through the Haight, Upper and Lower.

Alice liked having Wash by her side, realized how badly she needed him there. Not someone, but him. For some reason she had told him things, the sort of things that couldn't be answered with words, and she needed him to stay long enough to answer. She was sure he would, sure she would like the answers he gave. And if she was wrong, well, she couldn't be, she couldn't bear to think of it, he had come back to her and could not leave again, she could feel it already, the betrayal about to touch her now when things were so good, and she didn't know if she could face it if it actually happened, if she could live in the depths of such pain.

Without feeling pain we are not fully a part of the world, and without feeling pleasure the same. But to put it all on the page— Sherilee did not know if she could do that, only that she was bursting with words and feelings, and if one could capture the other she might succeed.

She wrote of a young woman in love who realizes in a meeting with a stranger that the man she loves will never love her, that he is, as long as she has known him, too much like the stranger, too much always someone she does not know walking into the room, seeing her as an intruder while she feels there is nothing he could do that would be intrusive.

The young woman runs, the stranger stays, and all the doors inside the house are shut, to be opened only by someone new.

The woman does not know where she is running, only that she must find someone like herself, that she must learn to take more than pleasure and that she may have to take it in the running, there may be nowhere to stop that is preferable to movement.

She will find something, although she does not know what. The wondering alone is better than it would have been to stay, thoughtless, in that strangely suffocating house, gradually losing herself as another possession of the man she thought she loved.

And she told herself she could not truly love that, what she now saw he was, but she knew that she had, and she had to find out why. Letting herself be controlled like that, the way she was ignored except for the little bits that fit his needs. But she also had taken from him only those parts she needed, only those parts she wanted to believe, not seeing that he held her not to nurture but to smother.

Not that he was to blame. They had been useful to each other. Their wants had been small and precise, and he had partially satisfied her desires, as she had partially satisfied his. And now, as a part of her past, he was even more useful.

As in one of those South American cultures that sees the past as before you and the future behind, she saw him clearly now and knew that she had to keep backing, that she could not control what she could not see and had to take care of only what she could. It was imperative that she step away from him. The future was unknowable, all she could do was back into it. Back out of one life, and into another.

Wash's explanation of searching for Sherilee had not assuaged Alice's anger. They had looked together one night, why couldn't they do it again? He told her there were things he was more comfortable doing alone, and she told him she was supposed to be one of his comforts. And he one of hers.

They were supposed to be doing something about their dreams together, and part of that was dropping the burdens of the past. Their lives had been killing them.

But San Francisco was one helluva place to be poor, so they'd better find those dreams fast.

She didn't know what had brought that up, they had never talked about money. Maybe that was why he thought they had to now. It must have crossed his mind, that they'd made no plans about how they would live, they were quitting one stage without knowing what the next would be.

She thought maybe she should go back to school, she hated school though, but maybe she could get a student loan, to get her through while she tried to find a dream she could reach.

And what did he think he'd do?

Wash didn't know, maybe the private eye thing. A long time ago he'd looked into how much it would cost to start up. Of course everything was more expensive now, and he didn't know if he had enough money saved. But anyway, it didn't seem like something he was really dying to do. There had to be something that was an honorable profession.

Alice didn't know about that. She remembered something she'd read in a music magazine, that once you take your singing out of the shower you're a whore.

And they'd both spent too much time in the seedy parts of town to bother defending that profession. Self-destruction wasn't the way out either of them sought.

Simon found Mercury in the second Haight Street club he tried. It was a hard rock hangout, filled mostly with longhaired men in jeans, and Simon's bedraggled appearance fit right in. There was one crowd along the bar, and a few feet past it another standing curiously on what would have been called the dance floor had anyone been dancing.

The place wasn't packed, and Simon's height lent him a clear view. He saw her near the band, swaying slightly, as they played their speed metal barrage. She stood next to a man about Simon's age, tall and gangly. Simon made his way between onlookers and yelled to her in greeting between songs.

Mercury smiled like she didn't mean it and yelled hello back, returned her attention to the band.

Taking her nearest arm above the elbow, Simon tugged on it gently and pointed his thumb backward, where it would be easier for words to be heard. The man beside her turned his face toward Simon's but Simon was looking down at Mercury. She patted the hand on her arm and he let go, and she walked in the direction he'd pointed.

She only wanted to know what he wanted, and if Richie had sent him why hadn't he come himself.

"Richie has nothing to do with it. I want to know about a statue, a missing statue. Of an ugly man."

"How should I know? If I wanted to rip off Richie, I woulda ripped off Richie. Not you. I mean, I kind of like your statues, they give me the creeps."

Simon glared.

Mercury shivered. "Not the kind of creeps where I'd steal. Then that cop showed," she said in a hurry. "It was like he was one of them. The statues, I mean. Only alive."

Simon knew without asking who the cop must have been. He asked for a description anyway. She didn't describe him well, but Simon knew. He could see the face.

He stood momentarily silent, the noise of the band fading into the distance. That bastard Wash. The sculpture may have been a part of them both, but it was a creation of *his*. And Wash had gone so far as to steal that.

Somehow he would get him. And through Alice, he grinned, might be the easiest way. He felt Mercury look at his face, ask what was wrong. He said thanks and turned away.

She watched him walk through the open door. Richie had stranger friends, she had thought, but that was before she saw Simon's face just now, changing like a series of masks.

CHAPTER 10
ALICE/SHERILEE

Alice lay awake in the dark bedroom, smelled the booze exuding from Wash's pores, felt the sweat on his body, listened to his rapid breaths as air whistled in and out of his mouth.

They had been up late, fatigued but filled with adrenaline and alcohol, and she would call in sick this morning, nurse him as much as he needed to be nursed, let that damned job she was quitting anyway discover what they'd be missing. She would stay where she was needed. Wash had come to her, at a time when she might have expected him to remain stoically alone, for last night there was little she could give him in the way of physical comfort.

They had talked, and gotten drunk, but he had stayed with scotch long after she had switched to water, and what she now felt upon waking early was not a hangover but a radiance, as though she had been placed here for a reason, as though, at least for a little while, things were as they were meant to be.

She got up, turned on the heater, put on a sweatshirt and jeans and slippers, and water for coffee. She did a quick face washing while the water boiled, thought of getting a newspaper but didn't want to leave him alone, in case he stiffened up and found it difficult to move. She would stay and bring him his coffee if that was what he wanted, or run him a bath if that was what he needed, or rub his back or help him out of bed or fix him some eggs…And damn, she bet he liked sausage. For that matter, so did she, but she couldn't eat much.

He was sure to sleep a little longer, she'd run out now and buy some. Alice stepped back into the bedroom and checked. The wheezing was as loud as before. The store was a few minutes away. She'd dash out and back before he woke.

She dressed, poured herself half a cup of coffee, drank it quickly, opened the front door and, as lightly as she could, shut and locked it.

She took one step down the hall and froze. Simon. He stood staring at her and she knew this was no coincidence, he was never up this early. He had not merely stepped outside his own apartment door, he had been waiting. He stepped toward her and she knew she had to get away. But she stood there, keys still in hand, knowing it would be useless to scream: Wash lay asleep in bed, probably unable to move.

Simon stopped right in front of her. Alice hoped her shaking didn't show through the thick, baggy clothes. Simon was asking her something, about Wash, and she didn't want to tell him. Wash was inside and too weak to defend himself and Simon looked crazed and she didn't want to tell him.

Then she realized what he had said, and she tried to keep the fear on her face, the fear she had been trying not to show. But it was hard not to smile. He was asking where Wash lived, not where he was. She figured she should put up some resistance, so she asked why he wanted to know. Simon's bloodshot eyes widened, and his giant hands grabbed her shoulders. Long fingers dug into her back and she felt herself being lifted from the floor. She gasped—her hands opened, keys dropped. Her back pressed against her door, she blurted out the address, as she had been willing to do all along, but her fear was no longer feigned. He let her go and Alice slumped to the floor. Neck tipped back, eyes and mouth opened wide, she squeezed her knees and watched Simon walk hurriedly toward the stairs.

She stood as soon as he was gone, let herself back into her apartment and waited. She wanted to make sure Simon was far away before she woke Wash.

To her surprise he laughed when she told him, said he could have his fucking statue and the whole damn apartment if he wanted it. They were starting over anyway, right?

And he told her how he'd stolen himself, Simon's clay vision of him, and said eggs would be fine, with sausage if she had it, and she groaned and shook her head and explained why she'd been in the hall, and Wash laughed again, then clutched suddenly at his chest, and as suddenly his hand was a fist and it jerked forward, away from his body. With coffee, then, he said as he unclenched his teeth, that would be fine, and if she'd give him the slightest hand he'd raise himself out of this supine position.

It was so simple for him. All he had to do was never return home.

Not living, she thought, had plagued her writing. It all had happened slowly, by gradations she had exposed less of herself, had ceased finding that which was new. As though something that had once been novel could remain that way.

Repeated even once...

Novel, now there was a word that meant less with each new one. New.

Sherilee could laugh, disparaging herself now, but wasn't she also disparaging others she had known? Even Otto? And the idea that she was criticizing not the man but only his work was absurd when dealing with a man who had put so much of himself into that work. Yet, if it was repetition, it was failure. And he could no longer redeem himself.

But failure, she smiled, was not such a bad thing. Not when an attempt had been made. And she knew there had been no lack of effort on Otto's part, or even on hers. The goddamn problem was finding something new. She had found a way to live that she enjoyed and had stayed with it, instead of breaking through it. Pleasure had led, inevitably, to tedium.

Sherilee drank a beer and wondered why, what there was about this she wanted to keep in her life, made love with Ron and wondered why (afterward), wrote words on paper and wondered why. It was not the pleasures themselves she wanted to change, but the circumstances under which they took place.

She wanted her love affair to endure, but stability was an offering too tempting in its comforts, too much like death. She needed evolution.

This was not expected to last. It might, but that would be a piece of luck. Making it last was not something she could try to do, she could only try to make it work. Continual discovery for one reduced the odds of permanence for two.

It was hard enough to live, harder still to live with a specific someone else, but it seemed she always needed someone. It was that there also always had to be change.

And though the change she sought was in herself, she could not change for anyone else.

Sherilee fucked Ron like the Earth was about to explode.

CHAPTER 11
WASH/ALICE/SHERILEE

WASH TRIED TO REMEMBER WHAT IT WAS LIKE TO WANT TO BE something, tried to remember when he was young. Boys' games, Robin Hood and cops and robbers, cowboys and Indians. Always wanting to be the bad guy. And never embracing anything else, enjoying sports but not being good enough at them to ever think he'd play in the big leagues.

In second grade he had liked a girl, and one of his friends had teased him about it, and he had beaten up the boy, and he had liked that too. He remembered few details of his youth, but the beating came back to him, punch by punch, and he couldn't help smiling at this recollection of triumph. Not proud now to be smiling, unable to understand how a brutal pride like that had stayed alive inside him.

All he'd learned to do in the meantime was manipulate people, and he didn't want to do that anymore. It was why he'd settled for something he was good at that didn't mean shit, because he didn't care if it did, he'd lost sight of that somewhere. But he owed it to Alice to introduce her to Sherilee. And he had seen a flyer promoting an upcoming show by Simon, and he couldn't help wondering if his head would be in it.

It was too damned early to be in a café, too early to meet a writer and a painter, too early Saturday morning for anyone who did anything on Friday night. But Wash had insisted Sherilee and Ron might be early risers, so here Alice and Wash had sat since nine o'clock, and Alice now nursed her second tall coffee as slowly as she could.

Wash was paranoid; it had probably served him well in his work, but she wished it was something he could drop now that he was unemployed.

She didn't know how long she could sit here but she knew she couldn't go away, not while there was a chance of meeting Sherilee Malcolm. Periodically she prodded Wash and he reassured her that Sherilee had come here before. But of course her habits could have changed, she might have decided she was attracting too much or not enough attention here, and his search would have to begin again.

Not that such a well-known person would be hard to find. Unless she was writing, holed up somewhere. She had been known to disappear for months at a time while writing a book. Still, if this Ron was her lover, Wash had been a little lazy tracking him down. He'd wanted it all to happen easily, as though an incidental event in his social life.

The truth was, Wash didn't have a social life. He knew how to get information from people, but he wasn't much good at having fun with them. So when information was hard to come by he would settle for drinking alone, something he was good at.

But last night he had stayed sober, and they had stayed home, at her place, and they had said little, comfortable sharing space, and they had done almost nothing but make love, slowly, as new lovers will, making discoveries.

His body still ached, and everything had to be done more gently than usual, and it had made a nice change, although she would be glad when the animal options returned. But the entire night had been more conscious, more aware. As though somehow she could get lost in that awareness.

It had been so long since she'd had a night like that: without words, without hurry.

Then the bastard had gone and set the alarm clock.

She forgave him in advance for getting up too early, although you'd think at least if he was going to do this he'd do it with anxiety and excitement and not as a precaution.

He was doubly forgiven when Sherilee Malcolm walked into the room.

Wash grasped one of Alice's wrists, held her in her chair, allowed Sherilee and Ron to order and receive their coffees, to turn and step toward an empty table.

Wash stood, smiled, and tipped his hat toward Sherilee, bared his bald head for her. She grinned and Wash took Alice's hand. Together they stepped toward Sherilee.

Wash began the introductions. Sherilee extended her hand to shake Alice's, looked at her for the first time. The hand dropped, the smile gone; Sherilee took a step backward.

All she had gone through had not prepared her for this, the meeting of her double, not when it had been such a doppelganger who had murdered Otto. This could be the one, she could not know, but this could be her. In this distorted mirror Sherilee saw with blinking eyes what others must have seen when they looked at her: a possible killer.

Sherilee wanted to turn and walk away, but she rooted herself in her spot, needed to be stronger than those who had thought her guilty, even if this so-called strength was only curiosity.

But knowing that she had not committed the murder, and that someone who looked like her had, she was unable to not suspect this woman, whose name she'd failed to catch, and to wonder why Wash was with her now.

Wash was some sort of detective, had implied he was a sleaze who did dirty work for lawyers, and was now casually having coffee with someone who not only looked like her but had gone out of her way to do so, the clothes the same style, the hair the same cut. She expected if she took out a cigarette this other woman would light it for her, and they would smoke together, cigarettes dangling from opposite lips at the same jaunty angle.

So she said excuse me, murmured something about a sudden chill, and held out her hand once more, this time shook the other woman's, and when she introduced Ron, the woman repeated her name. Alice. Ah, Sherilee smiled to herself. Through the looking glass I go.

And as she smiled, Sherilee realized that her tremor had surprised the remainder of the quartet, that she had put them ill at ease. Her smile broadened. She had gone from discomfort to control, and although tension continued inside her, it did not show as she led the trailing trio to a table for four.

Alice sunk into lip-nibbling silence as Wash explained with a slight stammer what a fan she was, hence the great resemblance. Alice emitted a couple of words of agreement on her own behalf, but that was all. Sherilee benignly granted them audience, wanted to know what this was all about, but assumed that asking would be the slowest route to an answer.

She wondered how Wash might orchestrate such a conversation, forcing the witness to break. Or if that was quite his line of work. It had to be. Somehow he tampered with witnesses, but he could not be allowed to leave a trace. She wondered how he changed a mind, how the snake crossed the grass unseen.

And she realized that if she needed his expertise, she should talk to him alone. In the meantime, the traditional meeting with the fan. Cordiality was in order, should it be that Alice had never killed anyone. And such politeness was the simplest of masquerades, coldly hiding the revulsion within. To possibly be at the same table with Otto's killer, without being able to know. Certain that such knowledge would lead to vengeance, that such a strength lay in her hands.

By all the morality she believed in, she would be compelled to murder the killer of a man she loved. She did not know if she could live with herself afterward, she didn't know if that was necessary. Only that someone had done something unforgivable, and it didn't matter whether vengeance was sweet. She lived with this hate.

My reputation does not matter. My reputation is not me. You can do nothing to me. Except that we are part of the same world, and when you rot your little corner, you rot a little corner of mine. I wish it were a distant corner, but you have come too close. You have hurt me, and it strikes me as immoral not to hurt you. Something must be done with you; your existence damages the world.

I am no avenging angel, there is nothing angelic about me. But I do not have the strength to join you in your Hell, to sacrifice myself, for there will always remain an iota of doubt, a possibility that you are not the one. And even if that doubt could be removed my strength might fail me. Then again, it might not. I would certainly kill you if you remained a threat to someone I love, but if you have done anything it is already done, and the only maternal instinct you have aroused in me is that of revenge, which perhaps not every mother holds dear.

You murder someone and you take the brutality out of murder. You blow a living human's head off and it winds up in a court transcript, it becomes paperwork. I went to a lot of trouble to get my head where it is; don't turn it into paperwork.

When you kill you deplete humanity, not of one life but of a feeling, a reverence for life.

Sometimes people have to kill; there are no absolutes. But love is not this great unbridled passion you seem to think it is; it is laden with mercy and kindness and compromise.

Having finished making a point, something about what art was supposed to do, Sherilee took a drink of her coffee, noticed it was no longer quite as hot as she preferred, and took another.

There was a gap in the conversation, and Wash filled it with a few words and the unfolding of a flyer from his pocket. *The Murder of Otto Workman* read the bold faced type across the top of the page, and beneath, *An Evening of Performance Art by Simon Parker*. Sherilee gasped. Ron looked about to as well, his eyes widening. Alice studied Sherilee's face but said nothing, looked grim and watched. Wash said it might be amusing.

Worse, Sherilee answered, it might be unavoidable.

Forced to believe in coincidence but not knowing how much there could be, Sherilee got Wash's number—Alice's number—determined to talk to him alone. She was on the other side of the window now, seeing a face much like her own, not a self she sought but a different self that sought her. This stranger, this Alice, wanted to become a part of Sherilee's world, wanted to find a way to make it part of hers.

It was not that Sherilee wanted exclusivity; she was even desperate to know this woman who might have killed Otto, to know whether she had killed him. But reticence remained, and initially it would be through Wash that she would seek information.

Wash could see himself self-destructing in some way, leaping in front of a car or through a window or off a bridge, his body no longer in his control. He realized there was a madness some-where inside him, something about himself he didn't trust, and that he had been keeping those thoughts at bay with alcohol. But now the alcohol didn't always work, madness would twist itself through the cracks, and he doubted that increasing his drinking would do anything but make him a pathetic drunk. Anyway, he didn't want to drink out of necessity. He wanted to enjoy it. Which would probably mean drinking less, and finding some way to live with those ugly aspects of his self.

He needed outlets for his insanity, and by quitting his job he no longer had them. Trapped inside him, lunacy did not wait, but sought a hole to burst through.

———

Another café, a different side of town, Sherilee and Wash alone. Wash's words began to ramble, he wondered about the possible imminence of death, whether there was such a thing as reincarnation, and if there was would a person who had not helped others in one life be sentenced to a next life of constant need?

It seemed improbable, he shrugged his shoulders, it sounded too much like that one big judgmental God he'd never been able to believe in—

—But, Sherilee interrupted, it might be the way the river flows—

She stopped, not explaining further, and he nodded his head in agreement.

Sherilee had come to grips with torrents of spiritual beliefs during her madness, and she did not concede that any one was more likely truth than any other, only that some provided better models for living, that a sense of eternity could open one's eyes to the brevity of one lifetime.

Or simply to the thought that getting by was akin to death, that to be alive meant to embrace life, not to shun it. That discoveries had to be made, luxuries forsaken, yet at the same time— again it came to her—life was incomplete without pleasure. But that is the form of incompletion some lives take, and to not understand and feel how that feels is also to fall short.

She asked about Alice. Wash explained her innocence, not that it was something he could prove but it was something he believed because he must believe, he did not know what he could do but hold this woman as his possible salvation, and not betray her.

—It would not be betrayal if she was guilty—

But it would, for he had made promises to her independent of the promises she had made to him, he had chosen to accept some things as knowledge without believing knowledge was possible, knowing doubt could always be found, that every perception was distorted. Every truth could be shown to be untrue with the properly pinpointed question or suggestion. It was his field of expertise: breaking people. And now he wanted to reverse field, to build someone up.

—But about Alice—

There was no evidence, only the word of a madman, a drunk. Police records were filled with professional incompetent witnesses. Some people will say anything, some people will see anything. Alice House had not killed anyone the night Simon Parker said she had because as far as anyone could tell no one had been murdered in San Francisco that night. There were no bodies found, there was no evidence of bodies removed.

—But that wasn't the killing—

She meant. She meant Otto Workman, and Wash knew that. But he didn't see Alice as obsessed with Otto, or so obsessed with Sherilee she would murder the man her idol loved most. Alice showed no signs of dementia, only of severe fandom.

—But he couldn't rule it out—

Only from what he knew about her, and getting inside people's heads was what he was best at. Not trust, but corrupting trust, and he trusted Alice. If she was a killer she was a stone cold sociopath and no one would ever know. And he didn't believe that. He always knew.

What he did not know was how he wanted to live. With Alice was the only answer, nothing else came to him. Perhaps in loving her he would relearn how to live, remember whatever it was he must have forgotten so many years ago. Something he might want to do, some way he could make a difference in people's lives. Right now he had guilt, without any sense of possible absolution.

And he had Alice with him, and she did not know what she wanted. It seemed to him some sort of journey must be necessary, things they had not yet seen might change the way they felt and thought.

It was a desperate need to escape, to get away from something without plans of getting *to* anything, and at this moment Wash thought that might be enough. There must be something in this world that would change him. He had to keep going until he saw it.

He knew his own feelings were tangled beyond recognition, processed to be made inaccessible, where they could not hurt him. And he wondered what this fear inside himself was, and he knew he had to allow himself to be touched, to be hurt, and the way he would most likely accept such transformation would be to find someone he could trust. For now he chose Alice, not knowing if she could be trusted, but knowing he needed someone in this role right now, and she was the one who was here.

Clutching at his still sore ribs he stood and steadied himself, shook free from this line of thought he must soon return to. He crossed the room and poured himself a drink, downed it in a gulp, relished the flavor and the effect. If only he could taste all of life this way.

He had to think about the people he had hurt, the lives he had left mangled. He had chosen Alice House as his reclamation project, but there were others, like Simon Parker. Perhaps not salvageable, and certainly less pleasant to attempt. But it was Otto Workman who was dead, not Parker, and Sherilee Malcolm who might have innocently paid the price, if Wash had not done what he had.

Not that Wash's motives had been so righteous, he had only been doing his job. He rarely did anything because it was the right thing to do, only because it was necessary. And he was not always proud of the necessities he gave in to.

CHAPTER 12
WASH

Trapped with memories of Simon's show, Wash sat, hot and bare-chested. He awaited Alice's return, a drink in his hand and the air conditioner on doing nothing for him. Wash had felt the show's direct hits, had even felt what he considered the misses, knowing he had driven Simon at least part of this way.

It had been over the top of course; it had been performance art. Simon had felt a need to be noticed, Wash could understand that, could see a variety of possible motives for the things done.

The depiction of Simon as victim and Wash as corrupter of truth, as though he could alter a fixed state.

Wash had no difficulty seeing this act as revenge and little more. But what Wash had seen had hurt. Appeasing, he realized, some of his guilt. Let the boy attack. Assail. A need to be knocked cold. Murdered.

This show of Simon's was a mixed media portrait of an impaling, but Simon was no Christ, he suffered because he couldn't do anything else. Yet he portrayed it as *The Killing of Otto,* and the suppression of someone trying to help, showing Simon as an innocent boy easily intimidated, leaving out the alternative: the weak-minded individual sending someone to die.

It was with this weak mind that Simon clung to the benevolent view of himself, failed to see his inept vision as a danger to society. He was incapable of recognizing himself as an imperilment to those he falsely accused. Ironic that his show contained so many mirrors, filled the room with distorted faces, many of them Wash's: what Simon saw so clearly was a reflection not of reality, but of his own confused mind.

It was Sherilee who was innocent. Wash knew that now, knew her. He hadn't known while helping her, he'd needed no certainty then, was only giving her a chance. Her constitutional right to a fair defense. The words meant nothing to him. He'd done it because it had been his job, and at the time he'd still enjoyed his work.

It was horrible the things he used to enjoy, but he knew it wasn't his fault that Simon was frail. Everyone got pushed off the edge from time to time, it was a question of how you landed. Wash had his own frailty, his own madness, but he didn't spend his time blaming someone for it. Insanity wasn't something that came out of nowhere. Simon had something wrong with him already, might have been insane before he "witnessed" any murders.

And there was some acknowledgment of that in the performance, his inability to reconcile what he felt with what he wanted to be. The demolition of the mirrors, and of the statues, rampant destruction, yet also the filming of those creations, and of their obliteration. He had to make what he had made, and he had to destroy it, but he still had to preserve those memories.

And he still was able to blame Wash, as though all was fine before his arrival. But you don't break mirrors because of someone else.

You also don't significantly change your appearance. Still, he thought, if changing your face means you can again look in the mirror, what you were sick of was only something outside. Yet, although some things were better in these fedora days, he still wanted out of most things he was in. Even this room, even this city, things he thought he loved.

He had to be hard to find, that was all. And except for Simon Parker, he had been.

So if Simon was trying to make him pay with pain...it hurt, but it was close enough to fair, it fit in the rules he'd always played by.

If Simon goes on to fame of some sort, leaves us all behind, then I'm the trigger, and whatever madness brings him greatness he should thank me for.

Madness. For it had not been only his art Simon had desecrated. His attacks were on others, one by one, those who had been his heroes—Sherilee, and a new statue, life-size, of Otto, smashed to the ground and pulverized with hammers—and of the man he saw as his enemy, Wash, whose bust Simon lifted above his head and flung, slammed against a brick wall, and, as it burst, fumes rose from it, spread through the room and temporarily caused everyone to choke, some with coughing fits before the air cleared.

Wash smelled the poison rising from the angry face, Simon like a stinking corpse, forced to walk and rot among us. Wash watched almost numb and heard Jimi Hendrix's *Freedom* blasting from overhead speakers. He was more relieved than surprised when Simon pulled from seemingly nowhere a large Bowie knife, ran it slowly across the back of one hand until it bled gently, then flashed it suddenly upward, the side of the blade glistening under a single bright light. Two strokes with an abrupt jerking gesture carved deep into Simon's cheek a garish red V. Simon screamed and fell to his knees, the knife dropping as both hands leapt to cover the wound. Blood seeped ceremoniously between his fingertips. Doctors and applause.

Wash finished his drink, considered hurling it through a closed window but felt too weary. This was not even a place he cherished. It should not be so hard to leave.

Waiting for Alice, Wash made a salad, stabbed it with his

fork. Finding pen and paper he scribbled down what came to him. He tried to see the words as form that could be drawn or sculpted. But it was only something garbled in his brain, no words got it right, it had no shape he could see.

Not meant for this, he again jabbed at his salad, poked the inanimate.

Jabbed in wait. Expecting, not knowing. She would be with him soon. And they would be gone. Together. But where?

She wanted to see New Orleans, it was beautifully decadent she said. He wanted only to drive. There would be stops along the way, he had to learn to stop and stare, time limits had to be removed.

Other limits too. She wanted to do things he wasn't ready for, things he didn't know if he could handle. She wanted to be tied up, she wanted them to go beyond any idea of love they thought they knew, but he didn't dare hurt her, didn't dare tie her up, didn't trust what he might do when she could not stop the thing inside him that, once started, he might be unable to stop.

He might tie her up and leave her there.

He felt his heart faster and faster against his chest. He needed to move, and he needed to lie still. Instead he got up and trembled, took off clothes, splashed cold water on his face.

Simon's implications could not be true, that he would do anything to prove he could do it, without further motive. That he so lacked any kind of identity he would do anything for the brief rush, and violent fantasies played into that arena of exhilaration. That he had beaten up Simon without any reason except it felt good. That he had saved Sherilee to prove he could save her, picked up Alice to prove he could, crushed Simon to prove.

Dropped Alice because he no longer had a reason to be with her, never had any desire to keep her, was a man without heart. And had taken her back fearing this realization, needed it to not be so.

Had a job of entering people's lives, altering them, and leaving. Always been alone, now afraid to be, but could not stop.

He didn't usually walk around naked. A chill went through him and he shook. Hurrying back to the bedroom he put on fresh dry clothes—T-shirt, jeans, and socks—then returned to his seat on the couch.

Unsettled by Simon's show, completely awakened, a triumph for Simon, Wash could not go on with his plans. He did not care about the answers to old questions. Guilt, liability. Had to get away from the old. Had to find something new.

Not knowing what a fresh start would entail. His hair was growing back, he would pay a barber to shave it again. For now he brushed his teeth, washed his face, put on his hat and shoes.

If he'd kept the job, he'd have killed Simon by now. Maybe Alice too.

I don't want to be awake, he thought, but I'm awake. Not much of a world where the only thing you want is out of it.

Wash crossed the room, found the bottle of scotch and took a slug. The shot glass, like all but some money and clothes, would be left behind.

Only what he needed for a long drive would come with him. Including madness.

He lurched again, stood, moved, not exactly walking but progressing forward, having forgotten how to take steps, forgotten how to restrain.

And he knew the kinds of promises he and Alice had made were not the kind they could keep. He knew it was getting away he needed, not getting away with her. She was a part of where he had been, where he still was. And he had to go someplace new. She did too. Not the same place. He liked her too much to bring her with him. No matter what she expected, no matter what he'd said, she'd be better off without him. She could live with the pain of this betrayal. Genuinely fond of her, he would not stop to brush his teeth, to wash his face.

Better this way. Found a cigarette butt in ashtray, kissed its lipstick stain, dropped it in shirt pocket. Moved hat from hand onto head, walked out door. Shut it behind him. Safer this way.

But stood in hallway shaking. Frozen. Forced his feet forward, legs as though asleep. Punched one and stepped, then the other. To the stairs. Held back tears, hand clenched rail, feet trudged down. One step. Then the next. Tears would not stay inside. Better for her. Alone. No other way. Expecting to fall with each step. Then, the next. Not used to being alone, but it's all he can ever be. No matter who is with him, no matter what he pretends.

CHAPTER 13
SHERILEE

THIS LITTLE ODE TO MADNESS, SHERILEE THOUGHT, IS AN ODE TO ALL of me, an ode to all that's missing. Fragments here and there, fragments form a whole, the hole that is me without you. Always dropping like rain seeking earth, something to seep into.

This little gift you give me, this gift of freedom, this gift of you not here, I wish I could give it back. I will join you in eternity but first I must join you in memories that always will haunt me, perhaps comfort me, but regardless are inescapable. I will see you in the movements of other men, I will hear your voice when another man's reply is lacking, I will turn on strangers for not being you yet occupying your space. I will become you for a moment and remove from the world all that does not deserve you. I will find you in all things and I will lose you in all things. I will touch you when you are not there because that is now the only way. And I know you will never leave me, however much I want you to, for you always had a way with exits and this is not the way.

And if it is up to me there is no redemption for the Hell-bound soul who took you, and if it is up to me you will rise to join me, but there are no incantations that will work, there is no undoing what has been done. None of this is up to me except how I deal with your absence, and I do not know how I will continue to mourn, only that I always will. And that this world without you is in its own state of mourning, your absence a sadness that no glare or haze can disguise. The inevitability that you would someday die in no way reduces the tragedy of your premature departure.

I think I have said this before, in other words, and in other words I will say this again, for however possible it is to live without you this is a circumstance too cruel, to you and to all who relied on you, and now I must find courage and display it so that I may be the object of someone else's reliance; to somehow take from you those inconsistencies I loved and provide for you a vicarious afterlife.

But again, why did the killer look like me?

There are murders solved and unsolved.

There is no truth.

It doesn't matter if what I saw in him was real. It was what I wanted.

Sherilee leaned forward, crying, crumpled into herself. She would always be alone.

It was what I wanted.

The End

ABOUT THE AUTHOR

 Rob Pierce wrote the novella *Snake Slayer*, along with the novels *Blood By Choice, Tommy Shakes, Uncle Dust,* and *With The Right Enemies*, the novella *Vern In The Heat*, and the short story collection *The Things I Love Will Kill Me Yet*. He lives in Santa Cruz, CA, with his corgi Misha and an oak cask of ennui.

To learn more about Rob Pierce and discover more Next Chapter authors, visit our website at www.nextchapter.pub.

Unforgiven Victims
ISBN: 978-4-82419-104-5

Published by
Next Chapter
2-5-6 SANNO
SANNO BRIDGE
143-0023 Ota-Ku, Tokyo
+818035793528

23rd February 2024

Milton Keynes UK
Ingram Content Group UK Ltd.
UKHW040653160324
439418UK00003B/22